"That baby

Dante sounded... actually wanted the baby.

A hollow feeling opened up inside Stella, a kind of longing. But she ignored it. "How do you know the baby is yours?" she asked.

He snorted. "Darling, you were a virgin. It's pretty much guaranteed that the child is mine." Intention blazed suddenly in his eyes. "But if you require a paternity test, let's take one."

The way he looked at her made her tremble.

What was wrong with her? So he wanted the baby. So what? It wasn't going to make any difference. He was still a mistake she had to correct. As soon as she figured him out.

"That won't be necessary," she said.

"Of course it won't," he echoed, something hard and certain in his voice. "Then again, it'll probably be one of the things I'll have to organize once we get back to my hotel, anyway."

Stella frowned. "What do you mean 'get back to your hotel'?"

Dante's dark gaze was steely and utterly sure. "I mean that I'm leaving and I'm taking you and my child with me."

Jackie Ashenden writes dark, emotional stories with alpha heroes who've just gotten the world to their liking only to have it blown apart by their kick-ass heroines. She lives in Auckland, New Zealand, with her husband, the inimitable Dr. Jax, two kids and two rats. When she's not torturing alpha males and their gutsy heroines she can be found drinking chocolate martinis, reading anything she can lay her hands on, wasting time on social media or being forced to go mountain biking with her husband. To keep up-to-date with Jackie's new releases and other news, sign up to her newsletter at jackieashenden.com.

Books by Jackie Ashenden

Harlequin Presents

Shocking Italian Heirs
Demanding His Hidden Heir

Harlequin Dare

The Knights of Ruin
Ruined
Destroyed

Kings of Sydney

King's Price
King's Rule
King's Ransom

Visit the Author Profile page
at Harlequin.com for more titles.

Jackie Ashenden

CLAIMING HIS
ONE-NIGHT CHILD

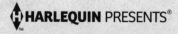 HARLEQUIN PRESENTS®

Recycling programs
for this product may
not exist in your area.

ISBN-13: 978-1-335-47853-5

Claiming His One-Night Child

First North American publication 2019

Copyright © 2019 by Jackie Ashenden

Printed in U.S.A.

CLAIMING HIS
ONE-NIGHT CHILD

To my dad. He'll probably never read this book,
but just in case he does... Hi, Dad.

CHAPTER ONE

As ONE OF Europe's most notorious playboys, Dante Cardinali was used to waking up in strange beds. He was also used to beautiful women standing beside said beds and looking down at him. There had even been a couple of instances where he'd woken up with his wrists and ankles still cuffed, the way they clearly were now.

What was unfamiliar was the barrel of the gun pointed at his head.

Dante had never been a man who cared over much about anything, but one thing he *did* care about was himself. And his life. And the fact that the beautiful woman standing over him was holding a gun in a very competent grip.

The same beautiful woman who'd been in the VIP area of his favourite Monte Carlo club and with whom he'd spent some time…talking…because he hadn't been in the mood for seduction—something that had been happening to him more often than not of late. It was a worrying trend if he thought about it too deeply, which he didn't. Because he didn't think about anything too deeply.

Whatever. He couldn't remember how long he'd spent talking to her, because he couldn't remember full-stop. In fact, he couldn't remember much at all about the evening and, given his current situation, it probably meant he'd blacked out at some point.

What he did remember was the beautiful woman's piercingly blue eyes, fractured through with silver like a shattered sky.

Those eyes were looking at him now with curious intentness, as if she was trying to decide whether or not to shoot him.

Well, considering his wrists and ankles were cuffed and he wasn't dead already, it meant there was some doubt. And if there was some doubt, he could probably induce her to give in to it.

He could pretty much convince anyone to give in to anything if he put his mind to it.

'Darling,' he drawled, his mouth dry and his voice a little thick. 'A gun is slightly overkill, don't you think? If you want to sleep with me, just take your clothes off and come here. You don't need to tie me to the bed.' He frowned, his head suspiciously muzzy but beginning to clear. 'Or put something in my drink, for that matter.'

The woman's cool gaze—she had told him her name but he couldn't remember it—didn't waver. 'I don't want to sleep with you, Dante Cardinali,' she said, her icy tone a slap of cold water on his hot skin. 'What I would like very much is to kill you.'

So. She *was* trying to kill him and she *was* very serious.

He should probably be a little more concerned about that gun and the intent in her fascinating eyes, and he definitely was. But, strangely, his most prevalent emotion wasn't fear. No, it was excitement.

It had been a long time since he'd felt anything like excitement.

It had been a long time since he'd felt anything at all.

He stared at her, conscious of a certain tightening of his muscles and a slight elevation in his heartbeat. 'That seems extreme.'

'It is extreme. Then again, the punishment fits the crime.'

The barrel of the gun didn't waver an inch and yet she hadn't pulled the trigger. Interesting. Why not?

He let his gaze rove over her, interest tugging at him.

She was very small, built petite and delicate like a china doll, with hair the colour of newly minted gold coins, falling in a straight and gleaming waterfall over her shoulders. Her precise features were as lovely as her figure—a determined chin, finely carved cheekbones and a perfect little bow of a mouth.

She wore a satin cocktail dress the same kind of silvery blue as her eyes and it looked like silky fluid poured over her body, outlining the delicious curves of her breasts and hips, skimming gently rounded thighs.

A lovely little china shepherdess of a woman. Just his type.

Apart from the gun in his face, of course.

'What crime?' Dante asked with interest. 'Are you Sicilian by any chance? Is this a vendetta situation?' It was a question purely designed to keep her talking, as he knew already that she wasn't Sicilian. Her Italian held a cadence from a different part of the country and one he was quite familiar with.

The sound of the island nation from where he'd been exiled along with the rest of the royal family years and years ago.

The island nation of which he'd once been a prince.

Monte Santa Maria.

'No.' Her tone was flat and very definite. 'But you know that already, don't you?'

Dante met her gaze. He was good at reading people—it was part of the reason he was so successful in the billion-dollar property-investment company he owned with his brother—and although this woman's cool exterior seemed completely flawless he could see something flickering in the depths of her eyes. Uncertainty or indecision, he couldn't tell which. Interesting. For all that she seemed competent and in charge, she still hadn't pulled that trigger. And if she hadn't done it now, she probably wouldn't.

He'd seen killers before and this woman wasn't one. In fact, he'd bet the entirety of Cardinal Developments on it.

'Yes,' he said, discreetly testing the cuffs on his ankles and wrists. They were firm. If he wanted to get out of them, she was going to have to unlock them. 'Good catch. I love an intelligent woman.'

She took a step closer to the bed, the gun still unerringly pointed at his head. 'You know what I love? A stupid man.'

Her nearness prompted a heady, blatantly sexual fragrance to flood over him, along with bits and pieces of his memory.

Ah, yes, it was all coming back to him now— sitting in his club in Monte Carlo, this pretty little thing catching his eye and smiling shyly. She'd been innocent and artless, a touch nervous and, despite her strongly sexual perfume, when she'd said it was her first time in a club he'd believed her.

He hadn't been in the mood for small talk but, as he hadn't been in the mood for seduction, and there had been something endearing about her nervousness, he'd sat beside her and chatted. He couldn't remember a single thing about that conversation other than the fact that he hadn't been as bored as he'd expected to be, as he so often was these days.

He was not bored now, though. Not in any way, shape or form.

She was looking at him coolly, like a scientist ready to dissect an insect, no trace of that shy, nervous woman he'd talked to in the club. Which must mean that it had been an act. An act he hadn't spotted.

Oh, she was good. She was very good.

His heart rate sped up even further, the tug of interest becoming something stronger, hotter.

Are you insane? She wants to kill you and you want to bed her?

Was that any surprise? It had been too long since he'd had any kind of excitement in his life, too long since he'd had anything like a challenge. The closest he'd come to interesting had been when his older brother Enzo had married a lovely English woman and Dante had been tasked with making sure Enzo's son behaved himself. A shockingly difficult task, given the boy had already decided that Dante was less uncle than partner in crime.

Dante had had to spend at least a week afterwards in the company of various lovely ladies simply to recover.

Marriage and children were *not* the kind of excitement he was after. They were too restrictive and far too…domestic for his sophisticated tastes.

Though, given the state of his groin, if a lovely woman could get him hard simply by waving a gun at him maybe his tastes had grown a little too sophisticated even for him.

Then again, it didn't look as though he was going to be able to escape any time soon, unless he charmed his way out. It wouldn't be the first time that he'd used his considerable physical appeal to manipulate a situation and this was a situation that definitely required some degree of manipulation.

And besides. It might be fun.

'Stupid, hmm? Maybe I am.' He allowed himself to relax, looking up at her from underneath his lashes. 'Or maybe I knew who you were all along and simply wanted to see what you wanted from me.'

Her lovely mouth curved in a faint, cool smile. 'I see. In that case, care to enlighten me on why you're here?'

Dante raised a brow. 'Isn't that your job? I'm still waiting for your villain monologue.'

'Oh, no, you apparently know all about it already, so don't let me stop you.' She cocked her head, the light gleaming on her golden hair. 'I'd like to hear it so, please, go on.'

Adrenaline flooded through him in a hot burst. This was getting more and more interesting by the second. And so was she, playing him at his own game. Little witch.

He allowed his gaze to roam over her, giving himself some time to collect his thoughts. If she wanted him to give her the run down on what he thought was going on so far, then he was happy to oblige her. Especially as he was starting to get some idea.

If she was from Monte Santa Maria—and that seemed certain—then the most obvious explanation for his current predicament was an issue with his family. The Cardinalis had once been rulers of Monte Santa Maria, at least until Dante's father had mismanaged the country so badly that the government had removed him from his throne and exiled their entire family.

Luca Cardinali hadn't earned them any friends during his troubled reign.

So, did that mean she was from a family whom Luca had wronged? She looked young—younger than he was—and he'd only been eleven when their family had had to leave, so she was likely to be someone's daughter.

He didn't remember much of his Monte Santa Mar-

ian history—he'd tried his best to forget about his
country entirely—but he seemed to recall an aristocratic family who'd been famous for their beauty, and
most especially their golden hair.

'Well, if you insist,' he said. 'Your accent is
familiar—from Monte Santa Maria, if I'm not much
mistaken—and, given your general antipathy towards
me, it's likely you're someone my father wronged at
some point.' He watched her lovely face intently. 'But
you're young, so I don't imagine Luca wronged you
personally, but your family. And, given your accent
again, I would say you're from one of the aristocratic
families. Probably...' His brain finally settled on the
name it had been looking for. 'Montefiore.'

Something in her shattered sky eyes flared. Shock.

So. He'd been right. How satisfying.

'Guess work,' she said dismissively, her chin lifting, her hold on the gun tightening. 'You know nothing.'

'And you are very good at pretending.' He smiled.
'If you're going to pull the trigger, darling, you'd better do it now. Or do you want the suspense to kill me
before you do?'

'You think this is a joke?'

'With that gun in my face? Obviously not. But, if
you imagine this is the first time I've woken up tied
to a bed, you'd be wrong.'

'This isn't some sex game, Cardinali.'

'Clearly. If it was, you'd be naked and so would
I, and you'd be calling me Dante. Or screaming it,
rather.'

A whisper of colour stained her pale cheekbones and he didn't miss the way her gaze flicked down his body and then back up again, as if she couldn't help herself.

Excellent. It would appear she wasn't immune to him after all.

His satisfaction with the whole situation deepened, not to mention his excitement. This was indeed going to be a lot more fun than he'd initially envisaged.

Her jaw had tightened. 'You seem very casual for a man who's about to die.'

Apparently she didn't like his attitude. Well, not many people did.

'And if I was really about to die, I would be dead already. But, no, you put something in my drink, dealt with my bodyguards, somehow managed to transport me to…' he took a brief glance around the room which looked like a standard five-star hotel room '…wherever this is. Cuffed me to the bed. Waited until I woke up, then started talking to me instead of pulling that trigger.' He allowed his voice to deepen and become lazier, more sensual. 'And, darling, considering that little look you gave me just now, it's not killing that you want to do to me. It's something else entirely.' He let his smile become hot, the smile that had charmed women the world over and had never failed him yet. 'In which case, be my guest. You've already got me all tied up. I'm completely at your mercy.'

Stella Montefiore had never thought killing Dante Cardinali would be easy. He was rich, important and more or less constantly surrounded by people, which made getting an opportunity to take him down very, very difficult.

But since she'd taken on the mission she'd spent at least six months planning how to get access to him and, now she had, her family was counting on her to go through with it. Especially her father.

It was a just revenge for his son's death and a chance to reclaim the lost honour of the Montefiores. It was also her chance at redemption for her brother's death, a death for which her parents still hadn't forgiven her, and she did *not* want to make any mistakes. There was no room for error.

In fact, everything had gone completely to plan, and here he was, at her mercy, just as he'd said.

So why couldn't she pull that trigger?

He was lying on the bed in the hotel room she'd managed to get him into with the help of the hotel staff, having told them he was drunk, and he was cuffed hand and foot. He shouldn't be dangerous in the slightest.

And yet...

There was something about the way he took up space on the bed, all long and lean and muscular, the fabric of his expensive black trousers and plain white shirt pulling across his powerful chest and thighs. Not to mention the lazy way he looked at her from underneath his long, thick, black lashes, the glints of gold in his dark eyes like coins on the bottom of a lake-bed. Completely unfazed. As if he dealt with guns in his face every day and it didn't bother him in the slightest.

And it didn't help that he was so ridiculously beautiful in an intensely masculine way. All aristocratic cheekbones, a hard jawline, straight nose and the most perfectly carved mouth she'd ever seen. A fallen angel's face with a warrior's body, and the kind of fierce sexual magnetism that drew people to him, whatever their gender.

She hadn't anticipated that, though she should have, given she'd put a lot of work into researching him.

In fact, there was quite a lot about Dante Cardinali that she hadn't anticipated, including her own response to him.

Her heartbeat was strangely fast, though that was probably due to the sheer adrenaline of the moment and the unexpected success of her mission, nothing at all to do with the seductive glint in Cardinali's dark eyes.

Not that she should be thinking about how seductive he was when she was busy trying to work up the courage to pull that trigger.

'In which case,' she said, trying to maintain her cool, 'Perhaps you should be begging for your life instead of making casual comments about me sleeping with you. Which, I may add, I would rather die than do.'

He laughed, a rich sound that rolled over her like velvet, all warm and soft with just a hint of roughness. 'Oh, I'm sure you wouldn't.' That fascinating hint of gold gleamed from underneath his lashes. 'In fact, give me five minutes and you'll be the one who's begging. And it won't be for your life… Stella Montefiore.'

Shock trickled like ice water down her back, smothering the heat his sexy laugh somehow had built inside her, and distracting her totally from his outrageous statement.

He knew her name.

Kill him. Kill him now.

Her palm was sweaty, the metal of the gun cool against her skin. She'd practised this, shooting at tin cans in the makeshift gun range her father had set up in the barren hills behind the rundown house they'd had to move into after her brother had been arrested, working on her aim in between shifts as a waitress at a local restaurant—the only employment she could get, as no one wanted to hire a Montefiore. Not when they were such a political liability.

But shooting a can was very different from shooting an actual man. A man who would have his life snuffed out. By her.

She swallowed, her mouth dry.

Don't think of him as a person. This is revenge. For Matteo. For yourself.

Yes, all she needed to do was pull that trigger. A muscle twitch, really, nothing more. And then all of this would be over—her father's quest for blood done, Matteo's death avenged and her role in it redeemed.

You asked for this, remember?

Her father had wanted to hire someone and she'd told him, no, that it was better for one of the family to undertake the mission, to minimise discovery, and that the person who did it should be her. He'd told her she was too weak for the job, too soft-hearted, but she'd insisted she wasn't. That she could do it.

And she could. It should be easy.

But still her finger didn't move.

'You're wrong,' she said, not quite sure why she was arguing with him when a single movement would solve all her problems. 'That's not my name.'

'Is it not?' His eyes glinted, the curve of his beautiful mouth almost hypnotising in its perfection. 'My mistake.' His voice was as deep and rich as his laugh and the sound of it did things to her that she didn't want.

The same things it had done to her all evening from the moment she'd seen him in the flesh and not as an image in a photo or an online video. She'd spent months studying him, reading up on his history, his lifestyle, his business practices and personality. Basically everything she could find on him, building up a picture of a dissolute yet charming playboy who seemed to spend more time in his string of clubs than he did in the offices of Cardinal Developments, the huge multi-national that he owned with his brother Enzo. He ruled the gossip columns and the beds of beautiful women everywhere, apparently.

'The world won't miss him,' her father, Santo Montefiore, had said viciously. 'He's selfish, just like Luca was. Another useless piece of Cardinali trash.'

Yet when she'd stepped into that club in Monte Carlo, sick with nerves—unable to adopt the veneer of icy sophistication she'd perfected to get past the VIP bouncer—and Cardinali had appeared out of nowhere telling the bouncer that it was fine and she could come in, it wasn't trash she'd been thinking of. Not when he'd smiled at her. Because it hadn't been a practised seducer's smile. It had been kind— reassuring, almost—and inexplicably comforting. In fact, he'd been kind all evening. He'd taken her under his wing, sitting her down in a quiet end of the club and getting her a drink. Then he'd sat opposite and talked easily to her about everything and absolutely nothing at all.

She'd been expecting predatory and cynical and he hadn't been either of those things. To make matters worse, she'd found him so utterly beautiful, so magnetic, so charming, that she'd almost forgotten what she'd come to do. He'd overwhelmed her.

The attention he'd given her had made her feel like she was the centre of the world and, for a girl who'd come second best most of her life, it had been an intoxicating feeling.

Until he'd looked at his expensive, heavy gold watch that highlighted the bones of his strong wrist and said that he was going to have to leave soon. And she'd realised that if she wanted to make a move she was going to have to do it then. One more drink, she'd said. Just one more. And he'd agreed, not noticing when she'd slipped the drug into it.

Cardinali was watching her now and the smile

turning his mouth wasn't kind this time. No, there was something else there. A hint of the predatory seducer she'd been expecting, along with a certain calculating gleam. Almost as if he now saw her as an equal and not the nervous, inexperienced woman she'd been in the club, or the soft-hearted, weak girl her parents had always thought her.

It made her heart thump hard in her chest, an inexplicable excitement flickering through her.

'My name is Carlotta,' she said. 'I told you that in the club.'

'Ah, then you'll have to forgive me my poor memory. Someone must have spiked my drink.' He shifted on the bed, as if he was getting himself more comfortable, a lazy movement that drew attention to his powerful body. 'So, are you going to stand there all night talking at me or are you going to murder me in cold blood? If it's the former, I hope you don't mind if I go to sleep. All this excitement is exhausting.' He shifted again and she caught a hint of his aftershave, warm and exotic, like sandalwood. It was delicious.

She took a steadying breath, trying to ignore the scent. 'Don't you care at all which one it is?'

'Since you're not going to kill me, not particularly.'

Her finger on the trigger itched. 'You don't know that.'

'Please, darling. Like I've already told you, if you'd really wanted to kill me you would have done it by now.'

He's right. You would have.

Except she hadn't. She'd told herself she couldn't shoot an unarmed and unconscious man. Plus, he needed to know why he had to die, otherwise what would be the point? But now he was awake and she wasn't telling him why he had to die. She was lying and pretending to be someone else instead.

What was she doing?

You don't want to kill him.

A shiver passed through her. She had to kill him. This was the job she'd undertaken months ago, for her father and for the sake of her brother's memory. For the honour of the Montefiores.

An eye for an eye. Blood for blood.

One of Luca Cardinali's sons had to die and, as his older brother Enzo was untouchable, that left only Dante.

Except...

His eyes were inky in the dim light of the room and they seemed to see right into her soul. There was no sharpness in them, only a velvet darkness that wrapped her up and held her tight.

'Lower the gun, sweetheart,' he said quietly. 'No matter what I've done, nothing is worth that stain on your soul.'

No, she shouldn't lower the gun. She needed to keep everything her father had told her about blood, honour and revenge in the forefront of her mind. She needed to be strong and, most important of all, hard. There could be no emotional weakness now.

And yet...her hand was shaking and she didn't understand why he should be so concerned with her soul when she herself didn't care about what happened to her after this was over.

'My soul is none of your business.' She tried to keep her voice firm and sure.

'If you're preparing to risk it to kill me, then it most certainly is my business.' His dark gaze held hers and there was no fear in it at all, only an honesty that wound around her heart and didn't let go. 'I'm not worth it, believe me.'

How curious. He made it sound as if her soul was actually worth something.

She should have shot him right then and there, but instead she found her hand lowering, exactly as he'd told her to.

He didn't glance at the gun, his dark eyes steady on her instead.

The weapon was heavy in her hand and she didn't understand why she hadn't pulled that trigger when she'd had the chance. Because now that chance had gone. The moment when she could have fired was lost.

You failed.

Shame rushed through her like the tide. How had he done it? How had he got under her guard? And, more importantly, why had she let him?

She'd worked hard ever since Matteo's death to excise all the soft, weak emotions inside her, the ones her parents had despised, and there shouldn't have been any room at all for mercy. But it seemed as if there was some small part of her that was still weak. Still flawed.

Anger glowed in her gut, hot and bright, over-whelming the shame, and before she realised what she was doing she'd put the gun on the bedside table and was bending down over him, putting one hand on the pillow on either side of his head. His hair was inky black on the pillows, his eyes almost the same colour as they stared challengingly back at her.

He smelled so good, the heat rising off him making her want to get close, to warm herself against him.

'What is it, kitten?' Dante murmured, staring straight up at her, gold glinting deep in the darkness of his gaze. 'Is it time to show me your claws?'

Again, there wasn't an ounce of fear or doubt in him, just as there hadn't been right from the start. He'd seen through her. He'd seen through her completely.

Her anger flared hotter, a bonfire of rage. How dared he find that weakness inside her? How dared he exploit it? And what was wrong with her that she had allowed him to do it?

Her perfectly executed plan was now in ruins and all because she hadn't had the guts to do what needed to be done.

Because, somehow, she'd let this man undermine her.

Well, if he wanted to see her claws, then she'd show them to him. And she knew exactly what to do to in order to cause maximum damage.

Her experience with men was non-existent, but she'd studied Dante Cardinali and she'd studied him well. Including what she could find on his sexual predilections. He was a man who liked being in control and who always, *always,* got what he wanted.

And it was clear that he wanted her.

Which gave her the perfect leverage over him.

'Not my claws,' Stella murmured, staring right back into his eyes. 'You can feel my teeth instead.'

Then she lowered her head and bit him.

CHAPTER TWO

THE LOVELY WOMAN who was probably Stella Montefiore, but definitely wasn't Carlotta, closed her teeth delicately around Dante's lower lip and every nerve-ending he had lit up with sweet, delicious pain.

He was hard instantly, his whole body tight, his wrists and ankles instinctively pulling against the cuffs with the urge to grab her, hold her.

He hadn't been expecting this particular move, though really the glittering flare of anger he'd seen in her eyes just before she'd bent her head should have warned him.

She wasn't as cool as she seemed, which was a delightful surprise.

In fact, the whole of her bending over him with that rich heady scent, her silky golden hair falling over one shoulder, her pale skin glowing against the fluid fabric of her blue dress, was a delightful surprise.

He'd been hoping for some fight and he'd certainly got it.

If only his hands were free.

Instead, he opened his mouth and touched his tongue to the softness of lower lip, a gentle coax.

She went still, her teeth releasing him, her lips a breath away from his.

So he bit her back, but not hard. A light nip to see what she'd do.

Her head jerked back and she looked down at him, her blue eyes glowing with anger, her cheeks pink. 'Damn you,' she whispered.

'Why?' His own voice had roughened. 'Because I stopped you from doing what you didn't want to do anyway? Because you're not a killer?'

She didn't reply, merely bent her head again, and this time her mouth was on his in a hard, furious kiss.

That she was inexperienced was immediately obvious, but she also tasted of anger and of passion, and his interest, already piqued, deepened even further.

He'd had inexperienced before, though he tended to steer clear of women who didn't know what they were dealing with when it came to him. He'd had plenty of anger before too, not to mention passion. But not all three at once, and not when the woman dealing them out had been on the point of shooting him in the head.

It made him even harder than he was already.

Still, that inexperience was a warning sign that this woman, no matter how cool and strong she seemed, no matter that she'd had him at gunpoint, had her vulnerabilities. And it was interesting that the mention of her soul had been the thing that had made her lower the gun.

But what had been even more interesting to him was the definite shame that had flared in her eyes after she'd put the gun down, only to be swiftly overtaken by rage. She hadn't liked failing her mission, that was for sure. And yet, instead of shooting him anyway, she'd kissed him.

Yes, that was very, *very* interesting.

Not only was she a woman with vulnerabilities, she also seemed to be a woman of strong passions. Which made for an intoxicating combination.

'Kitten,' he murmured against her mouth. 'Are you sure you know what you're doing?'

In response she bit him again, harder this time, the tips of her breasts brushing against his chest as she leaned in closer. Holy God, her nipples were tight and hard. He could feel them through the cotton of his shirt.

Lust uncurled in his gut, thick and hot, making him catch his breath.

It had been a long time since a woman had made him feel like this, he had to admit. And he wasn't a man who denied himself anything he wanted. Self-control was all very well in certain situations, but when it came to sex he would freely admit to being a glutton.

Then again, she'd had the gall to drug him then tie him to a bed, so why should he give her everything she wanted right now?

He moved his head on the pillow, pulling his mouth

away from her. 'Sweetheart, if you want that, you're going to have to ask for it.'

She made an angry sound and tried to kiss him again but he closed his mouth against hers.

The breath went out of her and she lifted her head. Her eyes were electric with anger, her cheeks pink. She said nothing, merely looked at him for a long moment. Then she straightened and took a step back from the bed.

But he didn't think she was going to move away. No, he'd seen something shift in that furious blue gaze of hers. She'd made a decision.

Anticipation coiled inside him, his breath catching yet again.

This woman was proving to be more and more intriguing with every second that passed and he couldn't wait to see what she was going to do next, how she would answer this particular challenge.

He didn't have anywhere to be or anything much to do beyond the usual round of PR work that he undertook on behalf of Enzo's and his company, plus the running of the more pleasurable side of the business, the resorts and clubs he owned all over the globe.

Anyway, he was bound to a bed. He couldn't go anywhere even if he wanted to. Luckily he didn't want to.

His lovely captor stood there a moment, her breathing fast in the silence of the room. Then she lifted her hands and pushed the straps of her silky blue dress off her shoulders, allowing the fabric to slide slowly down her body before pooling at her feet.

She was naked underneath it apart from the scrap of white lace between her thighs.

Okay, *that* was a move he hadn't anticipated her making. Not that he was complaining. Not in the slightest.

He'd seen a lot of beautiful women in his lifetime—more than he could count. But it wasn't this woman's physical beauty that felt like a punch to the gut, though she was indeed lovely: small, delicate and pale, her breasts the sweetest curves, her nipples pink and pretty.

No, it was the way she stood there with her chin lifted and her back straight, proud as a queen, her gaze full of challenge. As if she was daring him to break his bonds and come to her. Kneel at her feet. Worship her the way she was obviously used to being worshipped.

His pulse accelerated, the ache in his groin becoming acute. He almost jerked against the damn cuffs again, but managed to control himself at the last minute.

'Is this a request?' His voice was uneven even though he tried to mask it. 'Because, if so, it's a very persuasive one.'

She said nothing. Her hands went to her hips and very slowly she eased down the lacy underwear she wore then stepped out of it.

Dio, she was golden between her thighs too.

His mouth watered, his heartbeat hammering in his head.

What is it with you? It's not like you to let yourself get all hot under the collar for a woman.

It really wasn't. He didn't care about much of anything these days, but he found he cared about this. He wanted her hands on him. He wanted her skin against his. He wanted to be inside her. Preferably right now.

It was concerning. He didn't want to want anything at all.

He gritted his teeth, for the first time in a long while considering denying himself. Because he shouldn't care if she didn't touch him or kiss him, or get that delicious body on his. It shouldn't matter to him in the slightest.

If it doesn't matter, why are you even thinking of refusing her?

Dante had no answer to that.

He smiled, though for the first time in years it felt forced, more like a grimace than a smile. And he tried to make himself sound nonchalant. 'Well, don't just stand there, kitten. Come closer and let me see you.'

And perhaps she heard the strained note in his voice, because an expression that looked an awful lot like satisfaction flickered over her lovely face. Then she moved back over to the bed, clearly in no hurry at all, and looked at him very deliberately, the same way he'd looked at her. She was flushed now, the pink extending down her throat and over the pale curves of her breasts, and it deepened as her gaze dropped to where he was hard and ready and aching.

And stayed there.

Electricity crackled the length of his body.

What the hell was she doing to him? He didn't let himself get like this, not with anyone.

'I can get hard for any woman,' he murmured lazily, trying to keep the hoarse note out of the words. 'But it'll take more than you being naked to get me off.'

She gave him a brief, scorching glance. 'Who says I want to get you off? Maybe I just want to play with you.'

Sneaky kitten. So this was a power play, was it? She'd seen the general state he was in and thought she could take advantage, clearly.

Well, she could try. He might be finding it a tad more difficult to be his usual cool self, but when it came to bedroom power games he was the master. Even cuffed to the bed.

'Obviously I'm not going to object to that.' He let his voice get lower, become seductive. 'But, if you want to play, you'd better know what you're doing.'

'Who's to say that I don't?' She reached out and stroked lightly over the hard ridge just behind his fly.

More electricity crackled along his nerve-endings, the light brush of her fingertips maddening. Dante ignored the sensation. Instead, he gazed at her from beneath his lashes, letting the look in his eyes burn hot.

She was inexperienced—that kiss she'd given him had proved it well enough—and even though it wasn't something he'd normally use to his advantage, given the circumstances, beggars couldn't be choosers.

'That kiss for a start.' He let his gaze roam over

her, blatantly sexual. 'Best to know what you're get-ting into, darling. I'm a lot for a little kitten to handle.'

A deep-blue spark glittered in her eyes as she stroked him yet again. 'You're very arrogant for a man tied to a bed.'

'And you're very confident for a virgin.'

The deep pink flush staining her skin became scar-let, gilt lashes sweeping down, veiling her gaze and hiding her expression. And he was conscious of a very particular kind of satisfaction spreading through him. Firstly, for guessing right and, secondly, for the fact that he was perhaps the first man she'd ever touched like this. The first man with whom she'd ever been naked.

He normally steered clear of virgins, as he wasn't a man an innocent should get entangled with, but he couldn't deny that for some reason he liked the thought of this particular woman being a virgin. He liked it very much.

A virgin with a gun. How…intriguing.

'Don't be embarrassed, darling,' he said, watch-ing her intently. 'Even I was a virgin once.' Though, thinking back, he honestly couldn't remember how or when he'd lost it.

She didn't say anything for a long moment. Then suddenly she lifted her head and moved to the bed, climbing on top of it and straddling him. The weight of her was slight, but the heat of her bare skin seep-ing through his clothes was astonishing.

His breath caught as the blatant sweetness of her perfume surrounded him, but underneath that was something light and fresh, combined with the musk of feminine arousal.

Pretty, pretty kitten.

She rose above him, the pressure of her body against his groin an agony, the sway of her lovely breasts making his mouth go dry. Her skin was glowing, a sheen of perspiration at her throat, the look in her eyes all fire and challenge.

There was not a hint of shyness in her, or at least none that she let him see.

'I'm not embarrassed.' She reached for the top button of his shirt. 'Why would I be?'

Her naked heat had sharpened his hunger while her refusal to back down ignited something far hotter. Something he'd thought he'd killed long ago.

His determination to win.

He smiled, allowing some of his sexual hunger to show. 'No reason at all. But if you want to play with me then I do suggest learning the rules of the game first.' He paused. 'You don't want to lose on your first try, do you?'

For the merest second an uncertain expression flickered over her face. Then it was gone.

'But I'm not going to lose,' she said coolly, pulling open the buttons on his shirt one by one then spreading open the white cotton, baring his chest. 'I might be a virgin, but I'm not stupid. And a man is only a man.' She pressed her palms to his skin, the heat of her touch like a brand, her blue eyes burning into his. 'Like you said, Mr Cardinali. You're at my mercy. And there's nothing you can do about it.'

* * *

Dante laughed that intensely sexy laugh of his, the sound heating everything inside her to boiling point, making her skin feel hot and tight, as though she wanted to claw it off and step out of it.

He was giving her the most blatantly sexual look from underneath his lashes, all liquid darkness and heat, and the feel of his muscular, powerful body made her lose all her breath.

It wasn't supposed to be this way. Biting him, taking off her dress, touching him, was supposed to tease him, taunt him with what he couldn't have. Prove her strength to him and also punish him for making her lose her nerve so badly.

And yet the only one feeling as if all of this was a punishment was her.

She hadn't expected that bite to ignite something inside her. She hadn't expected his mouth to be quite so soft or for him to taste quite so delicious, like dark chocolate, fine whisky and all the seven sins rolled up into one.

She hadn't expected the way he'd looked at her naked body to make her feel as if she was going to burn to ash where she stood. Or that touching the hard length that pressed against the wool of his trousers would feel so astonishingly good.

She hadn't expected the intense throb between her thighs to be quite so demanding either.

Damn him. This was supposed to be a strong moment for her, not one where she felt as though she were standing naked in the path of an oncoming storm with nothing to protect her.

You've only got yourself to blame.

It was true. Sadly. She'd been the one who'd decided to bite him, to kiss him, to get naked and touch him. And now here she was, sitting on top of him, completely at the mercy of the desire inside her that had gripped her by the throat and wouldn't let go.

That wasn't supposed to happen. Sexual desire was supposed to be another of the weaknesses she'd cut out of her life. And yet his bronze skin beneath her palms was so smooth, the muscle under that so very, very hard, and all she wanted to do was press harder, test his strength, spread her fingers out and soak in all his heat.

But the hidden glints of gold in his dark eyes held her completely hypnotised and she couldn't look away.

'Poor kitten.' His voice was rough and deep, the rich amusement in it like a caress against her skin. 'You don't understand, do you? I'm not at your mercy. You're at mine.'

It seemed a ridiculously arrogant thing to say, when he was the one on his back and cuffed to the bed. Yet...

He was fluid and powerful underneath her, and hard, like granite carved direct from a mountain. She could see that power beneath her hands, feel it in the tight coil of his muscles and in the heat running through his body. It was there in his eyes too, an arrogant certainty of his power that made her want to tremble.

She felt that certainty within herself, in the desire that wound through her, exposing her. In the way her breath came short and fast, and in the relentless throb of heat between her thighs. In the tightness of her skin and the acute awareness of every part of her that touched him and every part of her that didn't. In the delicious, warm scent of him that made her mouth water and her heart beat faster.

You're weak. You've always been weak.

Stella shoved the thought from her head. There was only one answer to that and that was simply to be stronger. She had to be if she was to overcome the insidious dragging need to surrender to him and the relentless pressure of her desire.

Dante Cardinali had seemed to be a simple man. A man driven by the single-minded pursuit of pleasure, a slave to any pretty face that came his way.

But it wasn't him who was the slave. It was her.

'No,' she whispered, both to him and to herself. 'I'm not at anyone's mercy.'

'Prove it, then.' Deep in the velvet darkness of his eyes, golden fire burned. 'Get off me and walk away. Put on your dress and leave this room.' His hips lifted as he said the words, the hard length behind the wool of his trousers brushing up against the soft, sensitive tissues of her sex.

Pleasure bolted like lightning straight through her and she couldn't stop the soft gasp that escaped.

'Do it.' His voice was rough with heat. 'If you think you can.'

She could. Of course she could.

Except he was moving subtly against her and the rhythmic pressure against that aching place between her thighs was making her shiver with delight. She'd denied herself many things in the quest to become better and stronger than the girl who'd betrayed her own brother into prison, and that included physical pleasure. She hadn't thought she'd missed out on anything, but...

Get off him. Walk out. Deny him. That's what you were going to do, wasn't it?

Of course it was. And, yes, she would get off him. Right now.

Except...the heat of him, and the power of his body beneath her, and the gentle rocking of his hips were all mesmerizing and she didn't want it to stop.

You have to do something.

He wasn't expecting her to get off him. That was obvious. He was expecting her to stay, to be at his mercy, exactly as he'd said. And her body simply wasn't going to let her leave. Which meant she was going to have to do something else to prove her strength.

She shifted back on him, shivering at the brush of the fabric of his trousers against her. Then, with shaking hands, she pulled at the buttons of his fly.

He stilled, his big, rangy body tensing beneath her. 'Oh, kitten,' he breathed. 'I'm not sure that's a good idea.'

She ignored him, tugging down his zip and reaching inside his boxers. Her fingers closed around him and she blinked, her breath sticking in her throat at the feel of him in her hand. So long and hard and hot.

She pulled the fabric away from him, staring at the length she held in her hand, completely fascinated.

'Stella.' Her name this time, in a rough and hungry growl. 'I wouldn't do that if I were you.'

But it was too late. Backing down was an impossibility. It would make this entire evening an even bigger disaster, not to mention reveal the depths of her weakness, and she'd already revealed more of that than she wanted to when she'd put down her gun.

She lifted her gaze to his, the molten heat in his dark eyes making lightning crackle in her blood. 'What did you want me to prove again?' It was another challenge and she didn't wait for him to answer. Instead she lifted her hips and fitted that hard shaft of his against the entrance to her body. Then she lowered herself down on him.

The feel of him pushing inside her was exquisite. There was no pain, only a wonderful stretching sensation and a pressure that tore a groan from her throat.

His smile vanished, his mouth twisting into a snarl, a rough, masculine sound breaking from him as she slid down on him even further.

Then she had to move and she was helpless to stop herself, the urge overwhelming. Rising and falling on him, at first hesitant and uncertain, then finding a rhythm. He'd gone silent, his hips lifting with hers, the fierce hunger on his beautiful face holding her captive.

They stared at each other as pleasure began to unwind in a shining cord, wrapping around both of them and pulling tight. Getting tighter. Then tighter still.

Stella braced herself with her hands on his chest, the world narrowing down to the rock-hard body under hers and the astonishingly good push-pull of him inside her…to the coil of pleasure that was tightening and tightening and tightening.

Her skin felt raw and over-sensitive, the desperation inside her growing teeth. She hadn't thought sex would be like this, that she'd be so feverish and hungry. That she'd be so desperate.

The room was cool and yet she'd broken out into a sweat, her palms damp on his chest. A moan escaped her, because somehow he was dictating the pace now, the movement of his hips faster, her body trying to catch up, chasing some kind of glory she didn't understand and which agonisingly kept moving out of reach.

'Touch yourself,' he murmured, his rich voice rough with dark heat, no trace of the polished playboy in it now. 'Do it now.'

And she found herself obeying him without hesitation, driven by her own hunger, moving her hand between her thighs and touching her own slick flesh. And as she did so he lifted his hips, thrusting up hard into her.

Pleasure suddenly detonated like a bomb, and she

cried out, throwing back her head, feeling herself
come apart in the most incredible blaze of light.

Dimly she felt his body tense, another roughened
growl escaping him, but she couldn't seem to focus
on that, not when her whole body was busy being
flooded with such sharp, intense ecstasy.

As it faded, she fell forward onto his hard chest and
for a second or two simply relaxed there, her cheek
against his hot skin, breathing in the delicious scent
of sandalwood, salt and musk. It was like lying on a
rock in the sun and she wanted to close her eyes and
drift, listening to the strong, steady beat of his heart
beneath her ear. The sound was reassuring in some
way, as powerful and enduring as the sea…

'Kitten,' Dante Cardinali said, his deep voice echoing through her.

The delicious warmth was fading, the feeling of
reassurance going out like the tide, leaving her cold
and shaking, and not in a good way.

Her arms trembled as she pushed herself up and
met the darkness of his gaze staring back.

*What have you done? You were supposed to kill
him, not get into power games. And you definitely
weren't supposed to have sex with him.*

Shame flooded through her, crushing her. This
was a mistake. A terrible, terrible mistake.

'Stella,' Dante said.

But she couldn't stand being in this room a second
longer, surrounded by the ruins of her mission and
the evidence of her weakness.

She slid off him, pulling on her dress and underwear with shaking hands, pausing only to grab the little clutch she'd brought with her. Then she moved quickly to the door on legs that felt as if they might give way at any moment.

'Stella,' Dante repeated, more forcefully this time.

But she didn't turn. She couldn't bear to look at him.

She opened the door and fled, the sound of him roaring her name one last time ringing in her ears.

CHAPTER THREE

'WHAT DO YOU THINK, Dante?' Enzo asked. 'Do we want to go with Tokyo on this one or stick with the New York office's plans?'

Dante wasn't listening, too busy restlessly pacing around in front of the windows of the boardroom in Cardinal Developments' London office. Rain pelted against the glass, obscuring the view of the city below but, just as he wasn't listening to his brother, he wasn't paying much attention to the view either.

He was in England with Enzo to work out some of the details of a new project in the City, which had been hijacked by some disagreement between their people in New York and Tokyo, and quite frankly he didn't have the patience for either thing right now.

Not when his head was full of Stella Montefiore.

It had been over a month since she'd left him cuffed to a bed in that hotel room in Monte Carlo, running out on him mere minutes after the most un-expectedly intense sexual experience of his life, and to say he was annoyed about it would be to under-state things massively.

He wasn't simply annoyed. He was furious.

And he wasn't furious that she'd not only drugged him and cuffed him but then tried to kill him. No, he was furious firstly because she'd run out without even a thank you, and secondly because, try as he might, he simply could *not* stop thinking about her.

That brief moment of excitement and pleasure should have been more than enough for him. After all, there were a great many other lovely women in the world, so he shouldn't be fixating or caring about one particular woman.

But for some reason he hadn't been able to stop.

For weeks all he'd thought about was the feel of her tight, wet heat around him and the scent of her arousal, the unbelievable pleasure that had licked up his spine the moment she'd lowered herself down on him.

Of the challenging look in her beautiful eyes as her fingers had closed around him, upping the ante on their little game in a way he hadn't expected. Or the way that look had turned to wonder as she'd lowered herself down on him and the heat and the pleasure between them had taken hold.

He'd never seen that look on a woman's face in bed before and he'd been riveted. Caught too by the knowledge that she was experiencing this for the first time and he was the one who was giving it to her.

Maybe it was simply because she'd been trying to kill him that had heightened everything, including the pleasure.

Whatever it was, one thing had become very, very clear to him: given that she had in fact been trying to kill him, and that he had no guarantee she wouldn't try again, he couldn't simply leave her to run around on the loose.

So for the past month he'd spent most of his efforts on investigating her and, more importantly, finding her. Efforts that had all ended up with frustrating dead ends.

Until now.

'Dante, for God's sake,' Enzo said curtly. 'You're giving me a damn headache.'

Dante blinked then turned around, shoving his hands into the pockets of his suit trousers. Enzo was leaning against the long, sleek black table that dominated the boardroom, his arms folded, his golden eyes disturbingly sharp.

'Are you going to tell me what the matter is?' he asked. 'Or are you going to continue to pace around, pretending to be me?'

His brother wasn't wrong. Pacing was definitely Enzo's speciality, not Dante's.

With an effort, Dante tried to relax. He didn't want Enzo to know about Stella, not yet. His brother was happy for the first time in his life and Dante didn't want anything to worry him, such as attempts on Dante's life from enemies back in the old country.

Besides, Enzo would no doubt start taking charge of the operation if Dante did tell him, and there was no way Dante wanted him to do that. This was his problem and he was going to handle it his way.

Nothing at all to do with wanting Stella Montefiore in your bed again, naturally.

Naturally. He'd had her once. He didn't need to have her again, no matter how beautiful she was or exciting he'd found her. He just wanted her found, any threat she presented negated.

'There's nothing the matter.' Dante consciously tried to relax his tense muscles. 'Why would you say that?'

'Because you haven't listened to a word I've said and you're pacing around like Simon does when he's restless and wants to go outside and play.'

'Though presumably with fewer tantrums,' Dante muttered. He loved his nephew but, as Simon was only four, Dante didn't much appreciate the comparison.

One of Enzo's black brows rose. 'Is that a comment on my son's behaviour? Because if so—'

'Of course not,' Dante snapped, unaccountably irritable.

There was an uncomfortable silence as Enzo stared at him.

'What?' He stared back. 'There's no problem.'

'And our father is alive and well and ruling peacefully at home,' Enzo commented dryly. 'Tell me. And it had better be work related. Simon starts school in a couple of months and the last thing he needs is one of his uncle's scandals all through the media.'

Since Enzo had married Matilda six months ago, he'd got very protective of his little family. Annoyingly so, in Dante's opinion. His brother had never minded his affairs before, but in the past few months he'd turned into a damn prude. It was irritating.

Dante had managed successfully to build a life that consisted entirely of seeing to his own comfort and he was more than happy with the present arrangement. He did *not* want anything to change it.

'It's nothing that need concern Cardinal Developments,' he said, trying to find his usual casual smile. 'Or Simon. It's merely a distracting entanglement.'

Enzo frowned. 'That doesn't sound promising. She's not married, is she?'

'Brother, please. A married woman? It's like you don't know me at all.' There, that sounded more like his usual self, didn't it?

Enzo's gaze narrowed, studying Dante in that sharp way he had. 'You're lying.'

'I'm not,' Dante said with perfect truth.

'She must be very distracting to get you tied up in knots like this.'

Enzo didn't know the half of it, but Dante wasn't going to enlighten him.

It had indeed been Stella Montefiore who'd drugged him and cuffed him. As soon as he'd got out of the hotel room, he'd called his personal assistant and asked her to find out everything she could about the Montefiore family. She'd given him a complete dossier the next day and he'd spent most of the day going through said dossier, trying to work out why on earth Stella had targeted him.

Not that it was all that difficult to find out once he knew her family history.

The Montefiores had been one of the leading aristocratic families on Monte Santa Maria until Dante's father, the king, had been exiled.

After that, because the Montefiores had supported the old regime, they'd suffered a terrible fall from grace that had led to Stefano Montefiore sinking everything he owned into Luca Cardinali's plans to retake his throne. The family had been beggared and then, to add insult to injury, the authorities somehow had found out about Stefano's machinations. While Stefano had escaped being implicated, his oldest son Matteo had not. Matteo had been imprisoned, along with various other of Luca's supporters, and then, years later, had died while still incarcerated.

It didn't take a genius to work out why Stella Montefiore had been trying to kill him: she and her father wanted Dante's blood in return for the death of a brother and son.

It was a vendetta worthy of a Sicilian.

Except she hadn't gone through with it.

'You know how it is,' Dante said aloud. 'The right woman can be…lethal in certain circumstances.' Though not so much in his case, except for the lethal blow she'd dealt to his self-control.

Enzo lifted a brow. 'Is that a fact? Care to talk about this particular woman?'

Dante looked back blandly. 'Not really.'

'In that case, can I please have your attention concerning this—?'

Dante's phone buzzed in his pocket and he forgot about his brother entirely, pulling it out and turning round to look down at the screen.

It was a text from one of the private investigators he'd hired to locate Stella, giving him an address in Rome.

He smiled, an intense feeling he couldn't quite name filling him. It was mainly satisfaction, but there was something else there too. An undeniable, feral kind of excitement.

It had been frustrating not being able to find her, that she'd somehow managed to escape all the people he'd sent out looking for her.

But now, *now,* he had her.

She wasn't going to escape him again.

Seems like you do care about something after all.

Of course he cared when it was about his own life. Though what he was going to do with her once he'd found her, he hadn't quite decided. Probably, if he was feeling particularly merciful, he'd give her a warning that if she made another attempt on his life he'd report her to the police. And, if he wasn't feeling merciful, he might just call the police then and there.

That's not what you want to do to her...

Well, no, of course it wasn't. He wanted to punish her a little too, for how she'd taken up so much space in his head and for the sensual memories that had tormented him for the past month. The memories that she'd given him.

It wouldn't be a painful punishment, naturally, but she'd definitely scream. With pleasure.

'You're looking pleased with yourself,' Enzo murmured. 'Does this mean you're going to listen now or are you going to interrupt me yet again?'

'It means,' Dante said, putting his phone back in his pocket, 'that something's come up. Looks like I have to head back to Italy.'

'I see,' Enzo said dryly. 'Nothing at all to do with a woman, I suppose?'

He gave his brother a brilliant smile. 'Not in the slightest. You won't need the jet? Good. I'm flying out ASAP.'

Enzo snorted. 'What about Tokyo?'

But Dante was already heading to the door. 'You know what to do about Tokyo,' he said over his shoulder. 'Don't wait up, brother mine.'

It only took a few hours for him to land in Rome, but he was impatient as he went straight from the jet to the car his assistant had organised for him.

Dante had never bothered with his own car, or even his own home for that matter, preferring the number of hotel suites in various different cities that he kept for his private use. He didn't like to stay in one place for too long, as he didn't like getting too attached to anything, so hotels suited his impermanent lifestyle.

He gave his driver the address the investigator had sent to him and told the man to get there ASAP. The traffic as per usual was hideous, and Dante tried to curb his impatience but, as the driver turned down increasingly narrower sets of streets lined with rundown-looking apartment buildings, his impatience turned into uneasiness.

The area reminded him of the dirty tenements in Naples where he and his mother had ended up after she'd dragged him away from his father and Enzo back in Milan. She'd told him they'd be going somewhere exciting where they'd begin a new life. A better life far away from Luca's petty rages and selfishness. And wouldn't that be nice? No, he wouldn't have his brother, but he'd have her and wasn't that important? Didn't he love her?

Naturally, he'd loved her, so he hadn't argued. Not that he'd minded leaving his frightening father, but he'd been upset at leaving his big brother behind. He'd hidden his distress, though, as it had upset his mother and he hadn't liked upsetting her. Especially when it had made her drinking worse.

The driver pulled up onto the narrow footpath and gave a dubious look out of the window at the graffiti on the walls of the nearest apartment block and the garbage in the gutter. 'You want me to get your bodyguard, Mr Cardinali?' he asked, glancing at Dante in the rear-view mirror.

Dante snorted. 'Please, Giorgio. I was raised in the gutters of Naples. I think I can handle a few tenements in Rome.'

He pulled open the door and stepped outside, giving the area a quick scan, his unease deepening still further.

The Montefiores had little money these days, but as far as he was aware they were still on Monte Santa Maria. So why was Stella living here? Presumably because it was easier to hide in a slum, but still. Not a good place for the small, delicate, lovely looking woman he remembered from back in Monte Carlo. Then again, she'd seemed very capable with a gun, so maybe she was perfectly able to fight off all manner of thugs.

He approached the address the investigator had given him—a large and rundown apartment block—ignoring the group of surly youths standing around outside the door. One of them said something to him as he went past, but all he did was pin the boy with a look. He still remembered the street-fighting skills he'd learned back when he'd been thirteen and he'd been beaten up for the fifth time while his mother had done nothing, passed out from another of her drunken binges. He'd decided that night that he was sick of being the neighbourhood punching bag and so had gone out to find someone to teach him how to defend himself. That was the last time anyone had laid a punch on him.

The teenagers, making the right choice in deciding they didn't want to take him on, didn't say anything else, leaving him to enter the building.

It was dark and dingy inside, the lift out of order, half the lights in the lobby out.

He ended up walking all the way to the fifteenth floor, grimacing at the dirty floors, stained walls and huddled shapes of people in the doorways and clustered in the stairwells. It was all too familiar to him. It was the 'new life' his mother had promised him when she'd taken him away. Only it had ended up with her dead a few years later, and him alone to fend for himself at sixteen.

An old anger twisted inside him, but he ignored it, as he'd been ignoring it for years.

There was nothing to be angry about, not now. Things had turned out well despite that. Enzo had come for him four years later, and together they'd eventually claimed that new life for both of them. His mother would have been proud.

On the fifteenth floor Dante scanned the hallway for the number the investigator had given him and eventually found it right down the end. He paused outside the door, aware that there was some kind of complicated emotion burning in his veins. However, since he didn't care to examine his more complicated emotions, he ignored it, lifting his hand to knock hard on the door instead.

There was silence.

'I know you're in there, Stella Montefiore,' he said without raising his voice. 'So you'd better open up, darling. Or, if you prefer, I can get the police involved. I'm sure your father would love that.'

There was another brief moment of silence and Dante found his heart rate accelerating for no good reason that he could see.

He had his hand in his pocket ready to pull out his phone and call the police when the door suddenly opened, a small, fragile-looking woman in jeans and a faded red T-shirt standing in the doorway. Her golden hair was in a messy ponytail, loose strands hanging around her lovely, if rather pale, face. Familiar cool blue eyes fractured through with silver met his.

And desire hit him in the gut like a freight train.

'There's no need for that,' Stella Montefiore said calmly, looking for all the world like she'd been waiting all day for him to show up at her door unannounced. 'Though, if you're afraid to be in a room alone with me, then by all means call the police.'

Stella's heart was racing, fear coiling tightly in her gut. The hard edges of the door handle were digging into her palm, but she didn't want to let go. Given the weak state of her knees, she'd probably collapse onto the floor without support, and there was no way in hell she was doing that. And definitely not right in front of him.

He'd found her. Somehow, he'd damn well found her.

Dante Cardinali stood in the doorway of her grotty apartment, blazing like an angel sent straight from God, the reality of his physical presence hitting her like a blow.

In the past five weeks, when she'd gone over that night in her memory—and she went over it a lot—she'd told herself that what had happened between them was an aberration. A momentary weakness on her part, brought on by inexperience and a failure to prepare herself properly for what she'd had to do. She'd also told herself that she'd overestimated the intensity of his personal magnetism. But all it took was one look to know that, if anything, she'd underestimated it.

He was so tall and broad, lounging on her doorstep as though he was at one of his exclusive parties and not in a rundown tenement in the middle of the worst part of Rome. He wore one of those phenomenally expensive custom-made suits he seemed to favour, with a black shirt and a silk tie the same inky blue as the Pacific Ocean. Somehow, the colour made the deep brown of his eyes more intense and highlighted the smooth bronze skin of his throat.

She'd touched that skin. She'd stared into those eyes as he'd been deep inside her…

Her breath caught.

No, she wasn't going to think of that. She *couldn't* think of that.

You have to. Considering that *got you into the situation you're now in.*

The fear she'd been battling the past few weeks returned with a vengeance, wrapping long fingers around her throat.

How had he found her? She'd thought she'd been thorough in her efforts to disappear. Initially, after the panic of her failure to complete her mission had worn off and she'd had some time to think about her next move, she'd briefly debated the merits of returning to Monte Santa Maria. But had then dismissed it.

She hadn't been able to bear the thought of going home and confessing her failure, of having to deal with the weight of her father's disappointment in her. Of having to tell him that, yes, he'd been right to doubt her. That she hadn't been strong enough to go through with it after all. That he should have got someone else to do what she couldn't.

No, she hadn't been able to accept that. Matteo's death would go unavenged and, as it had been her and her stupid soft heart that had got him imprisoned in the first place, she couldn't give up after just one failure.

It was true that another attempt on Dante Cardinali's life would be that much harder, considering he'd be on his guard, but what other choice did she have? Failure was not an option, not again.

So she'd regrouped, texted her father that it was taking more time than anticipated but would all proceed as planned and started considering her next move. She'd shifted from place to place to hide her tracks in case Cardinali tried to find her, using nothing but cash in an effort to keep her digital trail to a minimum.

Eventually she'd settled on Rome as a place to lay low for a little while—the apartment she'd found pretty much as low as she could get—to give her time to figure out another way of getting close to him.

But first her cash had run out, then so had her luck, and now he was here because apparently she hadn't been as careful as she'd thought at hiding her tracks.

Yet another failure to add to the list.

The weakness in her legs threatened to move through the rest of her, making her tremble, blackness tingeing the edges of her vision.

Oh, God, please don't let her faint in front of him. She wouldn't be able to bear the humiliation.

'Ah, there you are.' His voice was as deep and as rich as she remembered and his smile was just as beautiful. But there was nothing friendly in it or in his dark eyes. 'You're a difficult woman to find.'

Stella clutched the door handle, blackness creeping further along the edges of her vision like a piece of paper held over a flame and slowly burning. She fought to stay upright, but the nausea she'd been battling the past two days—that wasn't the stomach bug she'd desperately hoped it was—shifted and she had to swallow hard against the urge to be sick.

His gaze sharpened, the smile turning his mouth vanishing. 'What's wrong?'

Damn. He'd noticed.

'Nothing,' she said thickly.

And then her legs gave out.

Dante moved, lightning-fast, and strong arms were suddenly around her, catching her before she hit the floor. Then she was being lifted as the man she was supposed to have killed gathered her tight against his hard, warm chest and kicked shut the door behind him.

Humiliation caught at her and she struggled, but he only murmured, 'Hush.' And, strangely, the will to protest faded, her energy dwindling away to nothing.

As if her body had simply been waiting for him to arrive and take charge.

Shame grabbed her by the throat, but the past few days had been a nightmare of exhaustion, illness and shock, and she just didn't have any strength left with which to fight.

Instead, she found herself relaxing against him and shutting her eyes, conscious of nothing but the warmth of him seeping into her and the iron strength of his body. For some reason there was something reassuring about it which should have concerned her if she'd had the energy for it.

What are you doing? What do you think is going to happen when he finds out?

Ice penetrated the warmth of his hold.

She couldn't handle this right now. It had only been two days since she'd finally forced herself to spend the last of her cash on a pregnancy test, and she hadn't had time to come to terms with the result herself.

She'd been halfway to figuring out a new plan but now that plan was in ruins as the consequences of her failure that night in the hotel room returned to haunt her.

It hadn't been a simple failure. It had been a failure of catastrophic proportions and she still hadn't figured out what she was doing to do.

But now you'll have to.

Yes, she would.

Dante put her down on the ratty couch in one corner of the living area and she found herself almost reaching out to hold onto him as the warmth of his body withdrew. God, she must be even weaker than she'd first thought.

Managing to stop herself at the last minute, Stella gripped her forearms instead as he stepped back, looming over her like a building, his arms folded over his broad chest, his gaze narrowed.

There was a moment's dense, heavy silence.

She steeled herself, ignoring the frantic beating of her heart and the nausea sitting in her gut, lifting her chin and arching a brow at him. She couldn't afford to show him any further weakness. She wouldn't. Her pride wouldn't allow it.

'What just happened?' he asked finally.

'Nothing.' She was pleased her voice was so steady.

'Nothing,' he echoed, disbelief dripping from his tone. 'Darling, you collapsed right in front of me.'

Stella gripped her forearms tighter. 'I'm tired. And I'm not your darling.'

'You look more than tired.' He studied her, his gaze uncomfortably sharp. 'You look exhausted.'

She decided to ignore that. 'So, are the police coming? Isn't that why you're here? To arrest me?'

There was another heavy silence.

'No,' he said slowly. 'I think not. I'll handle you myself.'

And despite her exhaustion and sickness a small, traitorous thrill shot through her, memories tugging at her again of his rock-hard body beneath hers and the length of him inside her, the intense, rhythmic thrust of his hips and how good that had felt…

What would it feel like if he actually had his hands free to 'handle' her properly?

Her mouth dried, her pulse accelerating.

Stop thinking about that. Focus.

Stella gritted her teeth, forcing away the memory, ignoring the throb between her legs that, given how sick she was feeling, shouldn't be there.

'How wonderful for me.' She tried for cool and managed to hit it. Mostly. 'And how did you find me?'

'Money. And a lot of people looking for you.'

He must have paid them a *lot* of money then, because she'd been very careful.

He really wanted to find you.

Of course he had. She'd tried to kill him.

'I see. In that case, congratulations, you've found me.' She gripped her forearms tighter. 'What exactly does the "handling" involve?'

Gold glimmered briefly in his eyes, a glimpse of the heat she remembered the night she'd tried and failed to kill him. 'You know, I hadn't really thought about it. But I'm sure we can work something out.' One corner of his mouth turned up in a smile that held a whole world of sensual promise. 'Can't we, kitten?'

Something inside her glowed hot in response, another helpless surge of desire.

No. She couldn't allow herself to feel this. She'd already made one catastrophic mistake. She wasn't going to make another.

Pressing her nails hard into her skin, she used the slight pain to chase away the heat lingering in her veins. 'I'll leave you my number then. Once you've decided how you want to "work that out" you can contact me. Until then…' she tried an icy smile '…perhaps you might want to leave?'

'Darling,' Dante purred. 'You really think that I'm going to simply leave now I've found you? After you tried to kill me? Who's to say you're not going to try it again?'

Stella swallowed, her mouth dry, the nausea roiling yet again. She should have eaten something that morning but she hadn't been able to face it. And now hunger was making the nausea worse. Her own stupid fault.

The fainting spell was bad enough, but throwing up in front of him would be ten thousand times worse.

'How about if I promise I won't do it again? Will that do?' She let go the grip she had on her arms, and tried to push herself to her feet, desperate for him to leave. But her legs were still wobbly and she swayed on her feet, dizzy.

Dante's sensual smile vanished and he reached out, putting his hands under her elbows to steady her, looking down into her face, his dark gaze sharp. 'You're not well. Kitten, what's wrong?'

She gritted her teeth against the sick feeling and the strange urge the concern in his voice had prompted, the urge to tell him everything, to let him deal with it. Because now it was his problem too.

But she couldn't. She had her plans and, though they might be in ruins now, there was a chance she could still salvage something from them. And if he knew that she was pregnant he might… Well, she had no idea what he'd do. She only knew that she couldn't risk him finding out.

'It's nothing.'

'It's not nothing. You can barely stand.'

His palms were warm against her skin and there was a part of her that wanted simply to stand there and rest, let him hold her up. A part of her she'd very purposefully excised from her soul years ago.

How ridiculous. What was he doing to her?

Forcing down the urge, she tried to pull away, only

to have his fingers tighten, keeping her where she stood. Probably a good thing, now she thought about it, because she had a horrible feeling she wouldn't be able to stand upright if he didn't.

The physical weakness made a hot, sharp anger wind through her. At herself for being so weak, and perversely at him, for being stronger than she was and making her so aware of that fact.

She knew she looked fragile, but she'd worked hard to overcome that by being emotionally strong. And the way he was holding her, with his palms resting under her elbows in support, made that strength feel brittle somehow. As if taking that support away from her would shatter her.

She hated the feeling.

'I'm fine.' She tried to gather enough strength to pull away from him. 'And I don't know why you're so concerned with my health. Don't forget I tried to kill you a month ago.' Might as well name it, as it wasn't likely he'd forgotten that particular aspect of their night together.

If he found that uncomfortable, he didn't show it, his gaze narrowing as he searched her face. Then his hold tightened and he eased her back down so she was sitting once more on the couch. 'Stay there,' he ordered.

Stella wanted to protest, but the sheer relief of not having to hold herself upright took all her energy, so she simply sat there as he turned and strode through the doorway that led to the tiny kitchen area.

Damn him. The last thing she needed was for him to be nice to her.

She leaned back against the couch and let her eyes close, exhaustion overwhelming her for a second. Part of her wanted to curl up and go to sleep, pretend the last couple of days had never happened. Pretend she hadn't slept with the man she was supposed to kill and wasn't now pregnant with his child.

Pretend he hadn't found her and that her plans weren't in ruins.

But that would be futile. All those things had happened—no point trying to convince herself otherwise.

The back of her neck prickled.

Her eyes snapped open.

Dante was standing in the kitchen doorway, staring at her. He was holding a glass of water in one hand and there was a curiously intense expression on his face.

A premonition gripped her.

He knows.

No, that was ridiculous. There was no way he could, not if she hadn't told him.

'What is it now?' She tried to keep her voice level.

Deep in his dark eyes, golden fire leapt, his jaw tight, his beautiful mouth gone hard. 'So were you going to tell me? Or were you simply going to get rid of it?'

All the air vanished from her lungs as shock washed over her.

'And in case you were wondering...' Dante raised

his other hand, a piece of paper in it. 'You left this on the counter.'

It was one of the pregnancy pamphlets she'd collected from the pharmacy where she'd bought the test.

Ice collected in her gut, making her feel even sicker, and for the briefest second she debated pretending not to understand what he was talking about. Telling him that those pamphlets weren't hers, but a friend's. Because if he knew the child was his...

It might not be the disaster you're anticipating. This could be the perfect moment to get close to him.

Stella held herself very still, examining the idea. Another attempt on his life was impossible now, because, as much as she hated to admit it to herself, if she hadn't been able to pull the trigger while he'd been lying there bound and helpless she wasn't going to be able to pull it at all.

But there might be another way to salvage her mission. A way to save herself from the failures of the past month and avenge Matteo's death. Redeem herself in her father's eyes, too.

Revenge. Make him hurt somehow, take away something he loved so he could feel the same pain as her family had at the loss of Matteo. It wasn't what her father wanted, but it was still something.

In fact, in many ways, having him remain alive yet broken could be even more satisfying than his death.

However, for that to work she would need to get close to him in order to find out who or what he cared most about.

So…perhaps she shouldn't deny she was pregnant after all.

Perhaps she needed to admit it.

And what about the child?

No, she couldn't think about the child just yet. Not making another mistake was the most important thing for her right now. She would think about the implications of her pregnancy later, when she'd completed her mission.

Stella forced herself to hold his furious gaze. 'I… hadn't decided.' She tried to keep her voice level. 'I only found out a couple of days ago.'

He said nothing for a long moment, but then he didn't have to. There was no trace of the charming smile she remembered. Or the warmth. Or the kindness. There was only anger burning in his eyes.

He's right to be angry with you. It's your fault, after all.

And it was. Her failure. She'd been the one who'd so given herself over to physical pleasure and wanting to prove something to him that she hadn't even thought about a condom. In fact, it hadn't been until she'd realised how late her period was that she'd even remembered she hadn't used one.

Despite her new resolution to finish what she'd started, heat rose in her cheeks, shame returning under the pressure of his black-velvet gaze.

He didn't say anything, moving over to the couch and stopping in front of her, holding out the water glass. 'Drink it,' he ordered flatly.

His tone made her hackles rise and instantly she

wanted to argue. But there was no point risking antagonising him right now. He might actually decide to leave and then she'd have to start all over again with a new plan, the opportunity she had now lost.

In fact, given how angry he was, that might still happen. He was, after all, a notorious playboy and an unexpected child wasn't exactly conducive to the kind of life he led.

No, she needed to be careful here.

Stella took the glass and sipped, the water cool in her dry mouth easing the nagging sickness in her gut.

He watched her, the look in his eyes burning. 'Well?' he demanded, the current of his anger running underneath the rich timbre of his voice like lava. 'Were you going to tell me you're pregnant? Answer me.'

'Yes, of course I was going to tell you,' she said coolly. 'Once the danger period was over.'

'So you're not planning on getting rid of it?'

The question set off a little shock inside her and she answered instinctively before she'd even had a chance to think. 'No. Of course not. Obviously I'm going to have it.'

'Obviously, you are.' The words were flat, the look on his face starkly uncompromising. 'Since that baby is mine.'

That little shock reverberated, stronger this time, reacting to something in his voice. He sounded… possessive, almost. As if he actually wanted the baby.

A hollow feeling opened up inside her, a kind of longing. But it didn't make any sense to her so she ignored it. 'How do you know the baby is yours?' she asked. 'It might not be.'

He snorted. 'Darling, you were a virgin. And, unless you went straight to another man's bed after our little interlude, it's pretty much guaranteed that the child is mine.' Intention blazed suddenly in his eyes. 'But of course, if you require a paternity test, then by all means let's take one.'

The way he looked at her made her tremble, though she didn't understand why, and she had to glance away to cover the momentary weakness.

What on earth was wrong with her? So it seemed as though he wanted the baby. So what? It wasn't going to make any difference. He was still a mistake she had to correct and she would. As soon as she'd figured him out.

'No,' she said. 'That won't be necessary.'

'Of course it won't,' he echoed, something hard and certain in his voice. 'Then again, it'll probably be one of the things I'll have to organise once we get back to my hotel, anyway.'

Stella frowned. 'What? What do you mean "when we get back to my hotel"?'

Dante's dark gaze was steely and utterly sure. 'I mean that I'm leaving in five minutes and I'm taking you and my child with me.'

CHAPTER FOUR

SHOCK WAS WRITTEN all over Stella Montefiore's lovely face, but Dante didn't care. He wasn't staying here longer than five minutes, not given the pallor of her skin or the dark circles under her eyes.

She needed rest and she needed it somewhere safe and that wasn't here.

She was carrying his child.

His child.

The reality of the fact was still echoing inside him like a bell being struck.

He'd seen the pamphlets on the kitchen counter as he'd got her a glass of water. Pamphlets with information on pregnancy.

And he'd felt something yawn wide inside him.

They'd only had sex once that night but... *Dio.* They hadn't used a condom. How was that even possible? He was fanatical about always using protection, but that night... He'd been drugged, had woken to find himself handcuffed to a bed with a gun in his face, only to be blindsided by desire for the very woman who'd threatened him. And she'd been so hot and he'd wanted her so very badly that it hadn't even entered his head to tell her that he had condoms in his wallet.

You fool.

She'd been a virgin. The onus had been on him and he hadn't even thought about it. And now look what had happened.

He hadn't been able to move for long moments, staring at those pamphlets, the realisation that she was pregnant and that the child was his slowly settling down inside him.

After the disaster that was his own childhood, he'd never wanted children for himself. Everything in life was transitory and painful so why not take as much pleasure as you could while you could get it? He couldn't do that with children and a family. In fact, the only family he'd allowed himself was Enzo—mainly because his brother refused to let Dante distance him—but that was it.

He didn't want anything else. He didn't need it.

So where the intense possessiveness came from that wrapped its fingers around his throat, almost choking the life out of him, he had no idea. But it was there, the need to grab Stella and take her away, keep her and his baby safe, impossible to deny.

It made sense in a way, since the woman had tried to kill him, which meant he couldn't trust her, let alone trust her with his child. Taking her somewhere where he could keep an eye on her seemed logical.

He was aware that he was trying to rationalise it,

but right now he didn't care. There was an unexpected biological imperative he was responding to and he simply couldn't stop himself.

Except it was clear that Stella had other ideas.

Her stubborn little chin had lifted and, despite her pallor, anger glinted in her silvery blue eyes. 'Go with you?' she asked flatly. 'I think not. But by all means, if you want to—'

'There will be no argument,' Dante interrupted, in no mood for protests. 'You're not staying in this hellhole and risking the life of my child.'

She gave him a look he couldn't interpret. 'Really? And since when does a notorious playboy give a damn about the life of his child?'

A memory shifted inside him, of that ghastly apartment in Naples—very similar to this one in Rome, now he thought about it—and his mother passed out on the couch, the sounds of someone shouting in the hallway outside. And he'd been terrified—*terrified*—that the person who'd been shouting would somehow break down their door and come in. And there would be no one to protect him…

A dull anger that had been sitting inside him for years, that he'd made sure to drown under alcohol and women and too many parties to name, flared to life, bringing with it a latent protectiveness.

His mother hadn't given a damn about *his* life. No matter how many times she'd slurred that she loved him, that she'd take care of him, she hadn't. She'd been drunk when he'd needed her, preferring the oblivion of the bottle to caring for him.

Do you want to end up being like her?

No. No, he did not.

Dante met her guarded blue gaze. 'Strangely enough,' he said, acid edging his tone, 'I find that I do give a damn. Unfortunately for you.'

Her expression turned contemptuous. 'Oh, please, don't tell me that the most infamous man-whore in Europe has had a sudden change of heart. Do the gossip columns know?'

He decided to ignore that, folding his arms and staring at her. 'Kitten, pay attention. Because I'm only going to say this once. You have five minutes to get your things and then we're leaving. And, if I have to pick you up and throw you over my shoulder, then believe me I will do it.'

There was a moment of silence, the tension between them gathering tight. Her eyes glowed, her beauty in no way dimmed by her obvious exhaustion. Neither, apparently, was her anger.

He didn't care. She wasn't staying here, not when she was pregnant with his child and he didn't trust her one single inch.

Nothing to do with how exhausted and sick she's looking.

Dante dismissed that thought. Yes, she wasn't looking well, but taking her away didn't have anything to do with *her*. He was protecting the baby. Plus, he really needed to deal with the question of her attempt on his life and whether she might have another go.

Stella's expression was still mutinous, and it was

obvious to him that she was trying to contain herself, but the silvery glow in her eyes gave her away.

Again, he didn't care. Let her be angry. This wasn't about her and this time it wasn't about him either. This was about their child.

Abruptly, she glanced away. 'Fine. I have nothing I want to take except my handbag on the table.'

Expecting more of a fight, Dante stared at her.

There was a set look on her face and she was holding her forearms tightly. Too tightly. Her nails were digging into her skin. And she'd gone white again, the circles beneath her lovely eyes like bruises. The strands of golden hair hanging around her face looked lank, as if she hadn't washed it in a while, and the jeans and T-shirt she wore were rumpled and stained, as if she hadn't washed those either.

A far cry from the perfect china shepherdess, in her blue satin cocktail dress and her perfect shining hair.

She'd been on the run, from the looks of things, hiding from him. Which meant that finding out she was pregnant must have come as a shock. Certainly enough of a shock that she hadn't been taking care of herself.

Something else shifted in his chest, that protectiveness again. But he didn't want to examine that feeling, so he didn't.

Instead, impatient all of a sudden, and suspecting that the reason she'd made no move to get up was because she couldn't, Dante bent and scooped her up in his arms once again.

'Stop,' she murmured, pushing ineffectually at him, while at the same time her body relaxed, as if his arms were the bed it had been searching for all this time.

That shouldn't have made him as satisfied as it did so he ignored that feeling too.

'Can you walk?' he asked instead, glancing down at her face.

She'd gone pink, which was a damn sight better than the pallor that had been there before. 'Of course I can walk.'

'Then do you really want me to put you down?'

Her mouth firmed and she glanced away again, staying silent.

Satisfied, Dante moved over to the table to allow her to grab her handbag, then turned to the door and carried her out of the apartment.

People stared at them as they passed, but he ignored the stares, just as he tried to ignore the slight, fragile weight of her in his arms. She was all softness and heat, and her scent was warm with a hint of feminine musk, no trace of the overwhelmingly sexual perfume she'd worn in Monte Carlo.

Which was good. Because his body, the traitor, was hardening at her physical proximity and he didn't need that on top of everything else.

In fact, he decided that, given how complicated this particular situation was, it would probably be best if he didn't further complicate it with sex. Denying himself didn't come easy to him, it was true, but there was a time and place for such things, and now was not the time and this was definitely not the place. Even his hotel was not the place.

Because she was not the woman he should be doing any of those things with, and certainly not after he'd already made the catastrophic mistake of having sex with her in the first place.

Ignoring the demands of his body, Dante carried her out of the building, conscious of the dealers and junkies in the hallways and the youths out on the pavement by the front. Giorgio had his wits about him enough to get quickly out of the car and pull open the rear door so Dante could put her inside.

'To the hotel,' Dante ordered shortly once Giorgio was back behind the wheel. And, as they pulled away from the kerb, an odd sense of satisfaction collected inside him. As if for once in his selfish, useless life he'd done something right.

Stella said nothing the entire trip, but he let her have her silence. She looked exhausted and for once he could think of nothing to say.

The hotel wasn't far from the Spanish Steps and the hotel staff, whom Dante all knew by name, were waiting to usher him to his usual penthouse suite.

He had a moment as he helped Stella from the car where he realised that there might be some curiosity about her, given she wasn't exactly dressed like his usual type of woman, and that wouldn't exactly be a good thing.

The Montefiores had fallen a long way since Dante's father had been exiled, but people might be curious enough about Stella to investigate who she was and why she'd suddenly turned up at Dante's side.

It wasn't a comfortable thought. He'd never cared about gossip—usually he openly courted it—but things were different now. He didn't want people drawing conclusions about her and he definitely didn't want anyone finding out about the baby. Not yet, at least. Not until he had some time to decide how best to proceed.

Ignoring half-formed ideas of getting someone to attend Stella, he decided to do it himself, pausing only to give the butler responsible for his suite instructions to bring up some food, while making sure the hotel staff knew to be discreet about Stella's presence, before dismissing everyone and shutting the door firmly.

Then he went into the luxurious living area where he'd left her sitting on the edge of one of the white linen-covered couches, gazing out over the fantastic views of Rome's ancient roof tops.

She wasn't sitting now, though. Clearly exhaustion had overtaken her because she was curled up, fast asleep, her head on one of the white linen cushions, her gilt lashes lying still on her pale cheeks.

Silently he went over to where she lay and looked down at her.

She seemed so small. A tiny, delicate china-doll of a woman with her big blue eyes and her corn-gold hair. A woman who'd first tried to kill him then given him one of the most intense sexual experiences of his life.

A woman who was now carrying his child.

The protectiveness that had washed over him at the apartment washed over him again, a rampant surge of emotion that he hadn't asked for, didn't want and yet couldn't seem to do anything about. It swamped him and he found himself grabbing the pale-grey cashmere throw that had been slung over the arm of the couch and tucking it securely around her so she didn't get cold.

For the baby's sake, naturally. He didn't much care about the woman who'd pointed a gun at his head five weeks ago.

So you do, in fact, care about the baby.

A certain tension settled in his jaw and in his shoulders.

He'd gone through life very happily not caring much about anything, so it came as something of a shock to realise that very much against his will he cared about this.

His child.

Back at that awful apartment where he'd found Stella, he'd thought it was simply about keeping that child safe. But, now Stella and the baby she carried were here in his territory, he was conscious that it went deeper than mere safety.

There was something else inside him, something he was pretty sure was that biological imperative operating again but, whatever it was, the fact remained that the baby mattered to him.

Of course it matters to you. Why else did you insist she have it?

The thought was sharp and deeply uncomfortable.

There had been a time once before when he'd walked away from a problem he hadn't wanted to deal with and he'd had to live with the consequences ever since. Consequences that even now he tried very hard not to think about.

So these days, whenever a situation looked like it might get complicated, he avoided it like the plague. Yet this was the very definition of complicated and for some reason he simply could not bring himself to walk away. Not this time.

The child hadn't asked to be born to a selfish playboy and a potential murderer. The child was innocent. And, if anyone knew what it was to be an innocent caught up in adult problems, it was him.

That baby needed someone to be there for it and, even though Dante knew he was possibly the worst man on earth to be a father, he nevertheless wanted that someone to be him.

Whether Stella Montefiore liked it or not.

Stella didn't want to wake up, but there was something delicious-smelling in the room. And for once she didn't feel sick. In fact, she almost felt hungry.

Except eating would involve having to open her eyes and she didn't want to do that quite yet.

She was lying on something ridiculously soft, and there was something equally as soft tucked around her, and she was warm, and moving felt like an impossibility.

Someone was talking nearby. A man, his voice

rich and dark and somehow soothing. He was speaking English and he must be on the phone since she couldn't hear any responses. Something about a child…

Reality hit her like a bucket of ice water dumped straight on top of her head.

The pregnancy test. Dante Cardinali coming to the door. Dante Cardinali finding out that she was carrying his child…

Every muscle in her body stiffened as that deep, beautiful voice rolled over her like a caress.

Him.

She'd been surprised when he'd insisted on her coming back to his hotel suite with him—she hadn't expected him to take responsibility for the baby quite so quickly, not a selfish, dissolute man like him. But it was all going to work very nicely for her plan, so she'd only put up a fight enough that he wouldn't suspect her motives. She'd even let him carry her to the car, nothing at all to do with the fact that she'd been too dizzy to stand.

Without moving, she lifted her lashes slightly so she could see where she was and what was happening.

It looked to be early evening, the pink light making the white walls of the room look as if they were blushing. The large glass doors of the living area were standing open to the terrace outside and there was Dante, standing with his back to her, one hand in his pocket, the other holding his phone to his ear.

She tried to muster some rage at him for the arrogant way he'd brought her here, as if he owned her, but her anger kept slipping out of her grip every time she tried to reach for it.

She was too warm and too sleepy, which was an issue when what she needed to be was cold, on her guard and wide awake.

He turned suddenly and his dark eyes found hers. And, just as it had back in that awful apartment when she'd opened the door to find him standing in the doorway, the impact of his gaze drove all the breath from her lungs.

He was smiling, but it wasn't for her, because as soon as he finished up the call and put his phone in his pocket the smile vanished.

A chill crept over her. It felt as though the sun had gone down even though rays of light were still filling the room.

'You're awake,' Dante said and it wasn't a question.

Since there was no point in pretending she was still asleep she sat up, pushing a lock of hair back behind her ear and drawing the soft wool of the throw around her. 'Yes. So it would seem.'

There was something in his eyes she couldn't read, something that made her uneasy. As if he'd made a decision about something. Had he changed his mind about the baby and called the police after all, perhaps?

No less than what you deserve.

Stella swallowed, fighting not to let any sign of her unease show.

'I had some food delivered.' He nodded towards the small stone table on the terrace, a couple of cushioned stone benches flanking it. The table had been set and there were plates of food on it, tea lights in small glass holders casting a golden glow. 'You should eat.'

It looked warm and inviting, and the smell of the food made her stomach rumble.

She gritted her teeth, instinctively wanting to refuse him yet managing to stop herself at the last minute. Letting him get to her would be a mistake and she couldn't afford any more of those. No, if she was going to figure out a new revenge plan then she had to lull him into a false sense of security, get him to see her as no threat. Which meant not fighting with him.

And you're hungry.

Yes, well, since the nausea had faded it appeared that she was indeed quite hungry.

Stella got up from the couch slowly, pleased to discover that her legs weren't as wobbly as they had been before and that she could at least stand up by herself.

Dante's gaze was completely and utterly focused on her, and she had the impression that if she fainted again he would probably know before she did and would catch her the very second that she fell.

She found the thought intensely irritating.

'I'm fine now,' she said shortly. 'You don't have to stare at me like I'm going to keel over any second.'

His gaze didn't waver. 'You said you were fine before and look what happened.'

'Again, you're very concerned about my health. Why is that?'

'You're carrying my child, kitten.' His expression

remained impassive, though there was an acid bite to his tone. 'If you hadn't noticed.'

Stella decided to ignore that for now, taking a couple of tentative steps. No dizziness threatened, so she took a couple more, moving through the doors and stepping out onto the terrace.

Dusk was settling over the city and, even though it wasn't particularly cold, she kept the throw wrapped around her. The air was full of the scents of the food on the table and the ancient city spread out below the terrace, plus the slightest hint of something warm and exotic. Sandalwood. Dante's aftershave.

He hadn't moved, yet somehow she'd got close to him. Which she hadn't meant to do at all. His gaze was very dark in the fading light, the sunset picking up the strange gold lights in his eyes and the odd golden glint in his thick, nearly black hair. That same golden light gilded his skin too, making him look like the angel he'd appeared to be back in that apartment.

A whisper of electricity crackled in the air between them, making her very aware of his height and the powerful body underneath all that cotton and wool.

You remember that body. You remember what it can do.

Oh, yes, she remembered. She remembered acutely. And she wished she didn't. In fact, that had been the one thing she'd wished many times the past five weeks. That she could forget what she'd done and most especially forget what he'd done to her.

You can't forget now. You'll have a reminder for ever.

Her hand had almost crept to her stomach before she stopped herself, though quite why she'd done it she had no idea. She couldn't think of the baby, not yet. Not when she still had a job to do.

Annoyed with herself and her physical awareness of him, she quickly stepped past his tall figure, moving to the table and sitting down on one of the cushioned benches. The food arrayed on small silver platters was simple but looked delicious: cheeses, olives, bowls of salad, hummus and some fresh crusty bread. There were cold meats too, but she couldn't eat that, or at least not according to the pamphlets.

A glass of wine had been poured for Dante, while orange juice in a tall glass stood waiting for her, condensation beading the sides.

She was desperately thirsty all of a sudden.

As she picked up the juice and took a sip, Dante moved to sit opposite, still watching her with that strangely focused look.

'How are you feeling?' he asked, picking up his wine glass and holding it loosely between his fingers.

'Fine. How long was I asleep?'

'A few hours.' His thumb stroked up and down the stem of his glass in an absent movement. 'You should eat. If you've been feeling sick, food will help.'

'I'm well aware of that, thank you.' She knew she should be good and fill her plate, not cause a fuss. But for some reason she felt stubborn and not inclined to do what he said.

Before Monte Carlo, she hadn't thought of him as anything but a target. And then, when she'd finally come face to face with the man, she'd had to think of him as a caricature rather than an actual person in order to do what had to be done.

But since the apartment, when he'd unexpectedly been protective of his child, she had the sense that perhaps he wasn't the caricature of the selfish playboy she'd turned him into. That perhaps there was more to him than she'd thought.

A mistake to think that, though. She could not afford to see him as a person. Once she started identifying with him, revenge would be beyond her, which meant it would be best not to feel anything at all for him. However, if that wasn't possible, then anger was her best bet.

He didn't appear to notice her being stubborn, putting his wine glass down, reaching for a plate and beginning to heap food on it. 'I know you can't have the ham, but you can eat all the rest.'

'So you're an expert on pregnancy now? Tell me, how many other children have you fathered?'

'Believe it or not, I have none,' he said calmly. 'And, as far as being an expert on pregnancy, my sister-in-law just gave me a quick rundown.' He sent her a quick, burning glance, the corner of his mouth turning up slightly. 'Don't worry, kitten. If I'm not an expert now, I will be by morning.'

She frowned, distracted from her anger for a moment. Dante Cardinali was famous for his determination not to settle down, no matter how many women had tried to make him change his mind over the years. At least that was what her research had indicated.

So why was he suddenly now interested in her pregnancy? And why had he been so quick to take responsibility for the baby back at the apartment?

She'd asked him about it back then, but he hadn't responded and she hadn't pushed, remembering that she wasn't supposed to rock the boat. But now… curiosity grabbed at her and she couldn't help herself.

'What does that mean?' She took another sip of her orange juice, the ice-cold liquid tart and delicious on her tongue. 'You can't tell me you actually want to be involved in being a father, or be desperate to settle down? And especially not with the woman who tried to kill you.'

Something glittered in his eyes and she couldn't tell what it was, though his voice when he spoke was mild. 'I don't know. Are you likely to try and kill me again?'

'I might.' She tried to echo his mild tone. 'I would advise sleeping with one eye open.'

He didn't say anything for a long moment and she found she was holding her breath, the hand holding her glass on the point of trembling. Then the sharp, glittering thing in his eyes faded, though the wicked glint that replaced it wasn't any better. 'Or I could just sleep with you and keep you thinking of…other things,' he murmured.

Unexpected heat rose in her cheeks, a gentle ache between her thighs, and try as she might she couldn't make either sensation go away.

'You're not going to try again, though,' he went on before she could speak. 'You weren't able to do it five weeks ago and I think it's highly unlikely that you'll manage this time round.'

He was right, but still she hated his arrogant assumption.

'How would you know?' she snapped before she could think better of it. 'You know nothing about me.'

'*Au contraire*, darling.' He put the plate he'd been filling with food down in front of her. 'I know quite a bit about you. In fact, in the five weeks I've spent hunting you down, I compiled quite the dossier.'

Sitting back, he picked up his wine glass again, the movement of his thumb on the stem oddly hypnotising. 'Stella Montefiore, youngest child of Stefano Montefiore. An avid supporter of my father's, even after our family was exiled. But then the Monte Santa Marian government found out about all the money your father tried to send mine, and all the plans they'd made to try and get his throne back. Yet for some reason they couldn't find your father. They could only find his son, Matteo. Who was the one who ended up in jail.' Dante's gaze was unwavering. 'And who died there.'

Old pain twisted in her gut, the guilt she'd thought she'd long put aside welling up and threatening to swallow her whole.

It was still there, that memory. Of the police coming to their house and demanding to know the whereabouts of Stefano and Matteo Montefiore. Her mother had wept incoherently, not able to tell them anything, which had only made them angry. And Stella had been terrified. She'd thought they were going to hurt her fragile, lovely mother, so she'd told the police what they'd wanted to know. That she'd seen her brother and father going down to the old caves by the beach near their house.

She knew that she shouldn't have told them anything, that she should have let her mother get hurt. That she should have let herself get hurt too, because the good of the family mattered more than any one person. Certainly more than herself.

But she'd only been ten and she'd always had a soft heart. She hated to see another creature in pain and it had been more than she could bear to hear her mother crying. So she'd told them.

And, while her father had managed to get away, her brother hadn't been so lucky. He'd been captured and had gone to prison, only to die there five years later.

It was her fault. All her fault.

She tried to hold Dante's gaze, to be hard and cold, the way her father had tried to drum into her to be. 'Yes,' she said steadily. 'He did. Your point?'

'My point, darling, is that I know why you tried to kill me. Your father wants an eye for an eye.' Dante swirled the wine in his glass. 'Or, rather, a son for a son.'

Of course. He wasn't a stupid man by any stretch.

Stella took another measured sip of her orange juice, using the movement to cover the harsh bite of guilt and anger. 'You seem to have all the answers.'

'But I'm right, aren't I?' He glanced at the plate she hadn't touched yet. 'Eat, kitten. Or I might be forced to make you.'

Oh, she would love not to. Or simply to push the plate away. But she wasn't supposed to be fighting him, and besides, she did need something to eat or else she was only going to feel more sick later.

Picking up an olive, she pointedly held his gaze, then put the olive in her mouth, the sharp, salty taste suddenly making her aware of how ravenous she was. Damn. She swallowed and picked up another. 'My dead brother is no concern of yours,' she said, trying to stay cool, if only to prove to herself she had no issue with talking about it. 'Or, if we're digging up dead family members, perhaps we can talk about yours instead?'

The research she'd done on him had delivered a few truths of its own. Such as the father who'd died in penury in Milan. And the mother who'd abandoned her husband and her other son, taking Dante with her when he'd been only twelve. She'd died too, or so the records suggested, of a head injury in a hospital in Naples.

Dante's gaze flickered at that, which meant she'd scored a point. Good. And then he said, 'You want to talk about my parents? Fine. My father was a power-hungry, selfish man who loved his throne more than his family and who spent the rest of his miserable life trying to get it back. My mother was a drunk who took me away when I was twelve in search of a new life. And we certainly found it in the slums of Naples.

She died when I was sixteen, leaving me to find my own way as a gutter rat. Which I did quite well until my brother Enzo found me.' At last, he lifted his glass and took a sip of the wine, watching her from over the rim. 'Any more questions?'

None of that came as a surprise to her—she'd known the facts. But he'd said everything so casually, as if none of it had touched him in any way.

She gazed back at him, curiosity tugging at her again. No, he'd sounded casual, but he wasn't. She could see the faint gleam of gold deep in his dark eyes. Was it anger? Pain? Or something else?

You're not supposed to be curious. He's not supposed to become a person to you.

He wasn't. And asking him questions about his past was a dangerous road to take.

Stella reached for a piece of the bread he'd cut for her, slathering some olive pesto onto it instead. 'No more questions. I have all that information already.' She took a bite of the bread, the sharp taste of the olive exactly what she'd been craving, then chewed and swallowed it. 'You're not the only one with a dossier.'

He lifted one shoulder in an elegant movement. 'In that case, why talk about the past? That's not what's important here. The important thing we have to discuss is what's going to happen with my baby.'

'*Our* baby,' she corrected before she could stop herself, a tiny shock going through her. Since when had she decided that the baby was 'theirs'?

Dante's eyes gleamed. 'Oh, so is that how it's going to be?'

'How is what going to be?' Tension coiled inside her.

'We've already decided that you're going to keep the child. But what happens now? Are you laying claim to it, kitten?'

Her hand had slipped to her stomach, as if she could somehow touch the baby inside her. The baby she'd tried very hard not to think about.

You will be a mother. How can you not think of that?

But how could she think of it? When she still had an important task in front of her?

Taking petty revenge while you have a life growing inside you.

Her throat tightened unexpectedly. It wasn't petty. Matteo had *died*. And he'd died because of her, as her father had never stopped telling her. It was up to her to make up for that death. To make it mean something.

She'd been the one to take on the assassination of Dante Cardinali and she'd failed. Which meant she had to be the one to try and salvage something from that failure. No matter what happened.

She would think about her baby afterwards. When she had the time and the space to concentrate. When Matteo's death had been avenged.

Until then she needed to give Dante what he wanted. Play nice, be meek, mild and biddable. And definitely don't argue with him.

Except that wasn't what happened.

'What if I did lay claim to it?' The words came out despite herself, torn from somewhere deep inside, the tiny part of herself that had remained the soft-hearted ten-year-old she'd once been. 'What if I did want my baby?'

Dante's gaze intensified. 'That, kitten, is a whole other conversation.'

CHAPTER FIVE

She looked so cool and untouchable sitting there staring at him, challenge in her eyes. Completely unruffled by his attempts to disturb her by talking about her family. Coolly telling him she'd probably try and make another attempt on his life. And then challenging his claim on their child.

As if she hadn't been the one to point a gun to his head the month before.

As if she hadn't been the one to take off her clothes and slide down on him, riding them both into the kind of ecstasy he'd only ever dreamt of.

Dio, it turned him on.

And it shouldn't, it really shouldn't. He'd already decided that he wasn't going to sleep with her, that it would make an already complicated situation infinitely worse, and yet…

She was so small and lovely, with the cashmere throw he'd tucked around her while she was asleep now snugly wrapped around her narrow shoulders. She had a bit more colour to her face, the shadows beneath her eyes less like bruises.

But the cool determination in her silver-blue eyes hadn't changed one iota.

Had what he'd said meant nothing to her? Not even the mention of her brother? He thought he'd detected a faint tightening of her mouth when he'd mentioned Matteo, and had experienced a fleeting sense of regret that he'd hurt her. Then again, she'd tried to kill him. And he'd wanted confirmation that she'd targeted him because of the blood debt incurred due to her brother's death.

She hadn't specifically answered that, but her change of subject had told him everything he needed to know.

Yes, he'd been right. Her brother had died, Stefano obviously held Dante's father responsible and he now demanded a price: Dante's life in recompense for the loss of his son's.

It was all very old school, and he might have found it amusing if the predicament he now found himself in hadn't totally been his fault.

But it was.

As much as he mightn't like it, Stella Montefiore was carrying his child. And he needed to make a decision about what to do.

He'd already decided that keeping her near was in his best interests, especially when he couldn't be sure she wouldn't make another attempt on his life, and he'd always been a fan of the 'keep your friends close and your enemies closer' approach.

But it wasn't just his life he was concerned about. It was the life of their baby too. He didn't trust her, which meant she wasn't going anywhere until the danger period of the pregnancy had passed. That would involve keeping her here, as he didn't want the media catching wind of it, plus he could ensure that she had the best medical care and treatment on hand should it be required.

Once the danger period was past, well…that was another discussion they would have to have. He certainly wasn't going to let her go free while she was still a danger to him and he hadn't seen any evidence that she wasn't.

It was either that or he called the police and he didn't want to do that.

They would find out who she was and then the proverbial would really hit the fan.

Since when have you cared what anyone would think?

Well, he didn't. It was his child that he cared about and he didn't like the thought of his son or daughter being born in jail.

Dio, he'd always thought that Enzo had gone slightly mad when he'd discovered he was a father, but now… Now Dante understood his brother in a way he hadn't before.

'And what conversation would that be?' Stella asked coolly. 'Is this the one we're going to have about what happens to our child when he or she is born?'

He stared back at her, just as cool. 'It's the one we're going to have where I tell you that when our child is born he or she will be staying with me.'

Oh, really? Since when did you decide that?

Apparently since right this instant.

Something flared in her eyes, anger probably. Good, let her be angry. She had to know where his line was and this was it right here. He'd lost both his parents—his father to his obsession with the throne, his mother to her obsession with the bottle—and that had been a painful lesson. And, even though he wasn't any better than either of them, he at least had the opportunity to do better, not to cause his own child that pain.

It was a surprise to him that he was considering someone other than himself for a change, but he didn't take the words back. He only met her gaze, letting her see the certainty in his own.

'You?' The word was layered with utter disdain. 'A reckless playboy who cares for nothing but himself? You seriously want your child with you?'

Her tone made his hackles rise, but he knew what she was doing. She was pushing him, just like she'd pushed him the night they'd met, which meant that he'd got under that cool veneer of hers in some way.

He smiled, relaxing against the stone of the terrace parapet at his back. 'You have to admit, it's better than having a murderer for a mother.'

She flushed, the anger in her eyes flaring hotter, and he could feel himself harden.

Dio, why did knowing he got to her affect him that way? Desire had got them into the situation they were in now and giving into it again would only make it worse.

'I know, kitten,' he purred, studying her face.

'You're not actually a murderer yet, but note that you did tell me to sleep with one eye open. And you have pointed a gun in my face and declared that you wanted me to die. The intention was there, no matter that you didn't do it.'

Her jaw had gone tight, her whole body stiff. Which was interesting. What didn't she like? Him pointing out what they both already knew? A sudden distaste about that particular word?

'What do you want me to say?' she asked tightly. 'That I'm not going to make another attempt on your life? Would you even believe me if I said it?'

Dante absently stroked the stem of his wine glass, noting the anger burning in her eyes despite her cool and contained veneer.

You don't believe she'd kill you.

Of course he didn't.

He knew sex. It was as close to a real connection with another person as he'd allow himself. Women showed their true faces to him in bed. When they were under him, transported with ecstasy, they allowed their souls to shine through and Stella had been no different.

He'd seen her soul that night in Monte Carlo and it was made of passion, joy and a wonder that had extended to include him.

It was not the soul of a killer.

He'd known it when she'd had the chance to pull that trigger and hadn't. And he'd known it the moment he'd watched pleasure overwhelm her.

But maybe she didn't.

'Put it this way,' he said slowly. 'I'd believe you. But I'm not sure you'd believe yourself.'

Shock flared in her eyes, a burst of bright silver as that cool veneer of hers cracked a little. 'What do you mean by that?'

'I mean, I don't think you're a murderer, kitten. I never have.' He studied her, fascinated by the gleam of emotion in her eyes that she couldn't quite hide. 'But you didn't like it when I pointed that out in Monte Carlo and I think you don't like it now. So you tell me. Are you happy to be called a killer, Stella Montefiore?'

An expression he couldn't name rippled briefly over her lovely face before she turned away, draining what was left of her orange juice. Her hand shook as she raised the glass—just a small tremble, but he noted it all the same.

Interesting. Did she really think she was a killer? Perhaps she'd had to tell herself that in order to go through with that first attempt on his life, and perhaps she had to keep telling herself that in order to finish the job.

Curiosity pulled tight inside him in a way he normally didn't allow.

How could this small, lovely woman, who seemed so delicate and vulnerable, who'd been nothing but softness and heat on top of him, think she was capable of taking a life?

Yes, she had a hard shell that she was clinging to for all she was worth, the veneer of the stone-cold killer. But that was breaking—even he could see that.

Was it he who was making it shatter? Or was it the baby?

An ache he didn't want to acknowledge tightened inside him, which he ignored.

'And I suppose you're fine with being called a self-ish playboy?' she said eventually, putting her glass down on the table with a click.

'That's not an answer.'

'Why should I give you one?'

'You don't have to.' He held her gaze. 'But I've seen your soul, kitten. You showed it to me that night you climbed on top of me and rode us both to heaven. And there's nothing dark in it.'

Why should it matter to you what she thinks about herself?

He wasn't quite sure. Maybe self-interest? After all, he didn't want her entertaining any further de-signs on his life. Then again, if he was so sure she wouldn't go through with it anyway, then what did it matter?

Perhaps this time it's not self-interest. Perhaps you care about her feelings.

Ridiculous. He barely even knew her let alone cared about her feelings.

Stella's cheeks had gone a deep pink, making the blue of her eyes more intense. And this time she didn't look away. 'If you think I'm not going to kill you then why am I still here?'

'You know why. The baby.'

'Strange that a selfish playboy famous for not settling down would suddenly be more than happy with an unexpected baby.'

There was a hot current of anger running through her voice, though she was clearly trying to keep it cool.

Yes, there was passion in her. Anger, stubborn will and fire enough to crack apart the fragile armour she was trying to hide behind.

What would it take to make it shatter entirely? And what would happen if it did?

The unwelcome pulse of desire that hadn't gone away no matter how hard he tried to ignore it beat harder, faster. Along with the tight coil of anticipation.

He shouldn't be thinking such things and he knew it. Temptation was something he'd never been very good at resisting, but he should be resisting it now.

Yet somehow he couldn't stop himself from baiting her.

'And I'm sure a killer such as yourself isn't best pleased to find herself pregnant either,' he commented. 'Surely it doesn't matter to you whether I claim my baby or not? After all, that'll leave you with more time to get on with killing and such.'

Silver flashed in her eyes, her jaw tight, tension in the line of her narrow shoulders.

It's wrong to push her and you know it.

Maybe he did. And maybe baiting her like this was a mistake. Then again, he'd made so many mistakes already, what was one more? Temptation had always been his downfall.

No, hunger for what you know you cannot have has always been your downfall.

The thought didn't make any sense to him so he ignored it.

'I will be a mother regardless of whether I'm happy about it or not,' Stella said fiercely. 'And, since I am, I will not shirk my responsibilities.' Her chin lifted slightly. 'This is my fault, after all.'

She looked so proud and serious and there was a certain kind of dignity to her. Like a queen nobly taking responsibility for the war she'd just started.

Ridiculous kitten.

This wasn't a war. This was a child.

'Really?' He swirled his wine in his glass, tilting his head and staring at her. 'So, in between drugging me and handcuffing me and pointing a gun at my head, then taking off your clothes and seducing me—while a virgin, I may add—you somehow should also have remembered to get a condom?'

The flush in her cheeks deepened even further. 'I'm not a child. I know about birth control.'

'Not, apparently, that night.'

Her eyes glittered. She was fragile and lovely sitting there wrapped in the soft cashmere throw, yet he could almost taste the sharpness of her fury. It poured through the cracks in her veneer like lava through the cracks in a volcano.

'Why are you pushing me like this?' she demanded. 'What's the point? You say you want our baby, but what does that mean? That you'll take it away from me the minute it's born?'

Dio, he wanted to see that veneer break apart completely, watch the fire he could see burning inside her leap high, the way it had done that night in Monte Carlo.

A mistake. Don't do it.

Except he couldn't seem to stop.

'And shouldn't I?' he shot back, putting his wine glass back down with a click. 'Don't you think that would be the best thing for the child?'

'No,' she snapped. 'I don't.'

'Then give me one good reason, Stella Montefiore.' He put his palms down on the table and half-rose to his feet. Then, very deliberately, he leaned across the space between them, getting closer to all that heat, to the fire that burned inside her. 'Give me one good reason why I should trust you with my baby.'

Stella had no idea why she was letting Dante Cardinali get under her skin so badly. It was only that the way he sat there, all lazy arrogance, secure in the power of his own charisma, needled her.

He seemed so certain of everything about her, firstly with his repeated references to her being a killer, and secondly by mentioning the fact that somehow, because they'd had sex once, he'd seen her soul. And then, to cap it all off, implying that she couldn't be trusted with their child...

She shouldn't let it matter to her, but it did. He might know about her family from what he could find on the web, but he didn't know *her*. And did he seriously believe she couldn't be trusted with a baby?

Yes, she might have been prepared to kill him, but she would *never* hurt a child.

Why does his opinion matter to you?

She couldn't answer that question and right now she didn't want to. She was too furious.

And it didn't help that she was *very* aware that he was the most phenomenally attractive man she'd ever seen.

He leaned across the table, the setting sun catching sparks of gold in the dark silk of his hair and outlining the strong lines of his handsome face. Close enough for her to see those very same golden sparks glowing in the darkness of his eyes.

Heat burned there, anger and a kind of demand that made something deep inside her clench tight with anticipation.

'Well?' he demanded, when she didn't say anything immediately. 'Do you have any answer to that at all?'

Of course she had an answer, but she didn't want to give it to him. She shouldn't have to.

Are you sure he hasn't got reason not to trust you?

Stella ignored that thought. The discussion was pointless anyway because, whatever he might say about the fact that she wasn't a killer, she still had a job to do. A mistake to correct. Matteo's death to avenge.

And everything had to wait until that had been accomplished.

So why are you arguing with him? You're not supposed to, remember?

Stella gripped the soft material of the throw draped around her shoulders, staring straight into the hot gaze of the man leaning across the table.

No, she shouldn't be arguing with him. She should be cool, calm and collected, ignoring him as if he didn't matter and nothing he said meant anything.

Because it didn't. He wasn't a person to her. He was barely even a man.

Except that was the problem, wasn't it?

Looking into his hot, dark eyes, feeling the spice of his aftershave and the warmth of his own personal scent wrapping around her, she couldn't think of him as anything but a man.

An overwhelmingly attractive man.

Her mouth dried and she knew she should look away, but she simply couldn't tear her gaze from his.

The atmosphere between them changed. Became electric, volatile.

All it would take was a single spark and the air between them would catch fire.

Stand up. Walk away. He's already got to you once. Are you really going to let him get to you again?

She couldn't. Yet her heartbeat was loud in her ears and her skin felt tight, prickling all over with the awareness of how close he was.

'Oh, kitten,' Dante said, a rough thread of heat running through his beautiful voice. 'You really need to stop me.'

She should. She wanted to. And yet…his mouth was very close, the shape of his bottom lip the perfect curve. She'd taken a bite out of it in that hotel room in Monte Carlo, testing the softness of it between her teeth. The taste of him had been delicious, a dark, rich flavour that she'd wanted more of. God, she could still remember it even now.

Her own mouth watered. All she'd have to do was lean forward and she could taste him again…

'Kitten.' He sounded even rougher now. 'You're playing with fire—you understand that, don't you?'

It took effort to drag her attention from his mouth, to meet the molten gold gleaming in his eyes, evidence of a desire he didn't bother to hide.

A desire that was just as strong as it had been five weeks ago and just as hot. And against which he was just as helpless as she was.

You could use that.

A hot burst of reaction shuddered down her spine.

And why couldn't she use it? She had no power here, no weapons of her own. She needed something. She hated the feeling of being powerless and weak. It made her feel like she was ten again, after she'd betrayed her brother to the police and she'd had to watch him be dragged away to prison. Powerless to stop it. Knowing she was the one to blame. Her and her soft heart.

She wouldn't be that weak. Not ever again.

Playing with fire? Dante Cardinali didn't know the half of it.

Stella didn't answer. Instead she leaned forward and pressed her mouth to his. She didn't know how to kiss, but that wasn't really the point. This was a power move, a rattle of the sabre. A declaration of war.

Her heartbeat thundered, his lips against hers soft and hot. She could almost taste him and it made her tremble, because there was a hunger inside her and it wasn't enough. She wanted more.

But he didn't move.

Wanting a reaction, she touched her tongue to his bottom lip, tracing the shape of it, exploring gently, hesitantly.

Still, he didn't move.

Frustrated, Stella pulled back. Perhaps she'd been mistaken? Perhaps he didn't want her after all?

But, no, there was fire blazing in his eyes and it nearly burned her to the ground.

'I told you that you shouldn't have done that,' he said.

Then abruptly he pushed himself away from the table top and straightened, moving around the side of the table with all the fluid, athletic grace of one of the great cats.

Excitement gripped her, the thump of her out-of-control heartbeat the only thing she could hear.

This time she was the one who didn't move, watching him come for her, his searing gaze holding hers. And there were no smiles now, no lazy, arrogant charm. The veneer of the playboy had been stripped away to reveal the predator underneath.

Perhaps she should have been scared, because he was very big and very strong, and she was far smaller than he was. But she wasn't scared. No, the opposite. She felt powerful. Because this was her doing. She'd been the one to strip that veneer from him, no one else. Just her. And with only a kiss.

It was intoxicating. She'd never felt so strong.

Dante stood in front of her for a second then, very slowly, he leaned down, putting his hands on the table on either side of her, surrounding her with the power of his muscular body and his heat, the heady spice of his scent.

'What,' he murmured softly, a dark threat in his voice, 'do you think you're doing?'

Stella lifted her chin, wild excitement careening around inside her, every part of her alive and aware of him and how close he was. 'What do you think I'm doing?'

His eyes glittered and for a second she saw the extent of his hunger stark in the inky depths, wide and deep and endless. It stole her breath. 'Don't you dare play with me,' he growled low in warning.

She shouldn't challenge him, not when it was obvious to her that he was close to some kind of edge. But she couldn't help herself. There was a hot tide of exhilaration washing through her and she couldn't shut herself up. 'Why shouldn't I play with you? Or can't you handle it when the boot's on the other foot?'

A muscle flicked in the side of his jaw. 'I can handle it.' The roughness in his voice was pronounced, a velvet caress that made her shiver. 'But you can't.'

She smiled, half-drunk on her own power over him. 'Oh, really?' she challenged, deliberating trying to incite him. 'Try me.'

The look in his eyes seared her. 'Be sure, kitten. Be very sure you know what you're doing.'

'Oh, I know. But I don't think you do…'

But she never got to finish, his lips coming down on hers in a hard kiss that stole the words right out of her mouth and the rest of her breath from her lungs.

It was hot and desperate, his tongue pushing into her mouth, demanding. Taking. But she didn't pull away. She lifted her hands and shoved her fingers into the thick silk of his hair, half-rising from the seat to kiss him back, just as demanding, just as hard.

Then he reached for her, lifting her, and plates were smashing, the sounds of glasses shattering as he shoved the remains of their meal off the table to clear a space. He placed her on the table in front of him, his hips pushing between her thighs, his hands sliding up her back. One hand tangled in her hair, tugging her head back, while the other shoved down the back of her jeans, his hot palm sliding over her bare skin and drawing her right to the edge of the table, pressing the damp heat between her thighs to the hard ridge beneath the wool of his trousers. And then he took control of the kiss and of her, utterly.

It was as if she'd unleashed a hurricane and she was standing right in the middle of the howling wind and driving rain, letting the fury of it buffet her. There was no fear, only an intense excitement and exhilaration, knowing she was the one who'd called this raging storm into being, that it was here because of her.

And she didn't know why that was so damn thrilling, but it was.

She curled her fingers into his hair, trembling as he took what he wanted, and she let him, her mouth opening beneath his, the heat and fire of his kiss igniting her. Turning her to flame so she was burning too, just as bright, just as hot. And she kissed him back, revelling in the rich taste of him, the wine he'd been drinking a subtle flavour that had her desperate for more.

He made a harsh sound, a kind of growl, the hand in her hair pulling harder so her head was drawn back, her throat exposed. Then he tore his mouth from hers, moving down to her jaw, raining kisses over her sensitive skin, nipping at the delicate cords of her neck, licking the pulse at the base of her throat that beat hard and fast for him.

Stella shivered all over, arching back to give him more access, his hot kisses a shower of sparks on her skin. It made her feel tight and hungry all over, desperate and hollow for something to fill her up.

Him.

But he was way ahead of her. He lifted his hands and gripped the thin, cheap material of her T-shirt and, without any effort, ripped the whole thing down the front, exposing her hot skin to the cool air. She gasped, shivering as his palms stroked over her stomach and then up, his fingers gripping the delicate lace of her bra and ripping that apart too.

'Dante.' His name slipped out on a sigh and then, as he shoved the remains of her clothing off

her shoulders and his palms found her bare breasts,
'Dante...'

He said nothing, his mouth at her throat, his
hands stroking and cupping her, squeezing gently,
his thumbs finding the hard buds of her acutely sensitive nipples and teasing them.

Stella shuddered, her mind going blank as his hot
mouth moved further down, finding one nipple and
closing around it, sucking hard. Pleasure exploded
brightly in her mind, a column of fire lighting her up
from the inside, burning away her resistance, burning away all thoughts of power and who had it, who
was weak and who wasn't. Of the revenge she had to
take and the baby she was carrying.

There was only this fire, this intensity, and the
pleasure that was burning them both alive.

It had been so long since she'd touched another
person, since she'd been touched herself, and her
hands found their way to his suit jacket before she
knew what she was doing, shoving it from his shoulders and then scrabbling at the buttons of his business
shirt, pulling them apart. Threads ripped, a button
or two pinging on the floor of the stone terrace, and
then his skin was beneath her fingers, smooth, hot and
hard with muscle. His head lifted from her breasts, his
mouth on hers again, the hunger in him demanding,
and she met it, pushing her tongue into his mouth,
exploring him with the same raw demand with which
he was exploring her. She shoved at the cotton of
his shirt, pushing that off his shoulders too, wanting
nothing between her palms and his hot skin. And,

God, he felt so good. So smooth and hard, with just the right amount of hair prickling against her palms, his muscles tightening as she stroked him.

She felt if she'd been drinking some incredibly delicious champagne that delivered only pleasure, and now she was completely and utterly drunk, and it was wonderful. There were no boundaries, no limitations. There was only this beautiful, *beautiful* man and his hands on her skin, his mouth on hers.

The man you were supposed to kill.

But she couldn't think of that, not now. There was an exquisite pressure building inside her and she was panting, his hands at the fastenings of her jeans, pulling them open. She wanted him to touch her so desperately that she thought she might cry if he didn't. And she never cried. Not since Matteo had been dragged away to prison.

Dante jerked her jeans off, taking her underwear with them, leaving her naked on the stone table, the remains of their meal surrounding them. The harsh sounds of his breathing filled the night and the dark fire in his eyes, the sharp, predatory look on his face, was all she could see.

He stood there shirtless, the setting sun gilding the hard, cut muscles of his chest and abdomen, and she couldn't stop from reaching out to touch him, her hands running lovingly over the width of his powerful shoulders and sculpted chest, his skin a perfect golden bronze.

He wasn't the charming playboy now. No, now he was pure predator, and he was starving for her.

She panted, reaching for the buttons on his trousers, wanting him, but he growled, knocking her hands away. 'No.' The word was bitten off and rough, and he took her wrists, guiding them behind her back and holding them there with powerful fingers. 'I'm in charge now, kitten. Not you.'

She struggled a little, purely for show's sake, because the feeling of being bound and held by him was like an electric shock straight between her thighs, increasing the already acute pleasure.

And he must have seen it, because he smiled fiercely, hungrily, an unholy light glittering in his eyes. 'You like that, don't you?' he murmured, running his free hand down her shuddering body, his fingers brushing through the slick folds between her thighs.

She groaned, wanting to deny it. Because of course she didn't like it when he was in charge. She wanted to be. Didn't she? And yet she couldn't the deny the electric pleasure of his touch and how it thrilled her that she couldn't move her hands to touch him back, at how she was at his mercy.

A shiver went through her and she gasped as his fingers stroked her wet flesh, finding the throbbing centre between her legs and gently stroking over and around, making her jerk and shiver in his arms.

'Please,' she gasped, pulling against his hold. 'Oh, please...'

There was a savage glint in his eye, a snarl twisting his mouth as he looked down at her. 'How does it feel to be held down, kitten? How do *you* like the boot being on the other foot?'

A thread of anger wound through the heat in his voice and the gleam of gold in his eyes, and she knew it was about the chemistry burning between them and how helpless he was against it.

But that only thrilled her, made her even more aware of her own power, and she arched up against his hand, pressing herself into his touch. 'Yes,' she moaned softly. 'More. Touch me more.'

He made a rough sound deep in his throat and muttered something vicious under his breath. But she was hardly listening, because then he was pulling open his trousers and pushing them down his hips, taking his underwear with it, and drawing himself out. Then he was urging her to the edge of the table, the furnace of his body pressed right to her bare skin. She groaned at the brush of his skin on hers, at the heat that felt as though it was burning her alive. And she was desperate to touch him, but his grip was too strong. Then he was fitting himself to the entrance of her sex and guiding himself inside, and she could feel the delicious, agonisingly pleasurable stretch of him as he began to push, her body giving way before his, adjusting to accommodate him.

She moaned, the harsh sound of his breathing filling the space between them.

He let her go for a moment, gripping her hips instead, angling her the way he wanted before drawing himself back and thrusting in again. Hard. Deep.

Stella gasped, reaching for his shoulders, her fingernails digging into his skin, revelling in the feel of the tense muscle beneath it.

He made a growling, masculine sound and thrust again, deeper, harder. The pleasure was irresistible, unstoppable, a force of nature she couldn't withstand or hold out against. So she didn't. She wound her legs around his waist and clung on to him, pressing her mouth to his throat, wanting to taste him, to get as much of him as she could any way she could get it. Because she was hungry for something she didn't understand, and the salt and musk of his skin was delicious.

She licked him, kissed him, nipped him, tasted him with every hard, deep thrust. Until his breathing became faster, harsher, and she found herself pushed down onto her back on the table top while he leaned over her, his hands gripping onto the opposite side of the table to give himself more leverage. The rhythm of his hips was hard and sure, his thrusts impossibly deep.

She'd never been to heaven before but she was pretty sure it was like this, on her back on a table, with Dante Cardinali's hard, muscled body inside her, over her, surrounding her in every way possible. His heat overwhelmed her, the subtle spice of his scent cut through with male arousal, and the evidence of his desire for her was in every line of his perfectly handsome face.

He looked like an angel in the process of falling,

his features taut and hungry and desperate, a feral light glinting in his eyes.

And she was the one who'd driven him to this point. She was the one who'd made him fall.

She couldn't remember why she was doing this or what point she had to prove any more. There was only him and the sharp intensity of the pleasure slowly ripping her apart.

The orgasm came like a bolt of white lightning, electrifying her, lighting her up from the inside, and she screamed with the pleasure of it. But he didn't stop, he kept on going, forcing her higher, making everything inside her tighten once again before another impossible release.

She called his name, shuddering against him as it detonated inside her a second time, turning her hot face into his neck as the aftershocks rocked through her, feeling him move even faster, a wild rhythm that she couldn't match this time. So she let him go, let him take what he wanted until he groaned, hoarsely muttering something in her ear as his big body shook with the force of the pleasure that was turning them both inside out.

Afterwards there was a long period of silence, the sound of the city below the terrace going about its business as if nothing had changed. As if she hadn't been given a taste of the power that lay in her own femininity. A power she'd never understood even existed until this moment.

Then Dante moved, his hands coming to rest on

the table on either side of her head as he pushed himself up a little, staring down at her.

Heat glowed in his eyes, the aftermath of pleasure and something else.

Fury.

'What are you doing to me, Stella Montefiore?' Dante demanded, as though all of this was her fault. 'What *the hell* are you doing to me?'

CHAPTER SIX

DANTE'S HEART WAS beating so fast it felt as if it was going to come out of his chest, the remains of one of the most intense orgasms he'd ever had making his head ring like a bell. He'd never had a response like this to a woman before and he couldn't work out what the hell was going on.

He'd told himself he wasn't going to make an already complicated situation worse by having sex, that he'd simply ignore the desire he felt for this impossible, lovely woman. But apparently he'd severely underestimated his own need to shatter that cool exterior of hers, get a taste of the passion that flamed beneath it. Slake the sudden, overwhelming hunger that had risen inside him the moment she'd laid her mouth on his.

Dio, he'd lost control, and he never lost control. Not like this.

Beneath him, Stella's gaze was wide, the flush that ran the entire length of her beautiful body making the blue of her eyes seem electric. She was looking at him as though she'd never seen anything like him

in her entire life, and despite himself it made satisfaction clench tight inside him.

Because there was no trace of the cool, hard
woman who'd sat opposite him just before, ignoring the cracks in the ill-fitting suit of armour she
wore. No, there was only this woman instead, soft
and passionate and hungry, with wonder glowing
in her eyes.

Then the wonder faded, her gaze flickering. 'I'm
not doing anything to you,' she said thickly.

Disappointment caught at him, though he had
no idea why. Because since when had he wanted a
woman to look at him the way Stella had just now?
He'd never wanted it. He'd never wanted anything
from a woman at all and he shouldn't be wanting
anything now.

'Liar.' The word came out in a growl, his anger
deepening for no good reason. 'You've been pushing me since the moment you got here.'

'And don't tell me you don't like it,' she shot back,
silver-blue glimmering up at him from beneath her
silky golden lashes.

Oh, yes, definitely her armour was firmly back in
place. Little witch.

He was still inside her and her body was soft underneath his. He could feel her inner muscles clench-
ing around him, and that and the heat of her bare
satiny skin along with the scent of sex was making
him hard again.

But, despite the challenging look she'd just given
him, the shadows beneath her eyes had got more pro-

nounced and there was a certain vulnerability to the curve of her bottom lip.

She was not only inexperienced but also pregnant and physically fragile and he'd just taken her roughly on the table. And, even though they were high up and probably no one would have seen, they were still outside and visible.

What were you thinking?

A certain tightness gathered in his chest. Since his mother's death he'd avoided taking responsibility for anyone else's wellbeing but his own, and it had never bothered him before. But, as it had back in her apartment, the urge to make sure Stella was okay tugged at him in a way he couldn't ignore.

'Did I hurt you?' he asked, searching her face for any signs of discomfort or pain.

She blinked and glanced away. 'No. I'm fine.'

He didn't think she was, though, because there was still a vulnerable look to her mouth and she wouldn't meet his eye. Reaching out, he took her chin in his fingers and turned her face back to his so he could see her expression. 'Kitten, you need to tell me if I hurt you,' he insisted. 'Because, believe it or not, that's the last thing I want to do.'

Her throat moved and he could feel the tension in her jaw, as if she wanted to pull out of his hold but was resisting it. 'I said I'm fine,' she repeated, glaring at him. 'And, no, you didn't hurt me. Okay?'

Which should have relieved him but didn't, because there was an undercurrent of anger in her voice that he didn't quite understand.

But now was not the time to push, so he said nothing, carefully pulling out of her. Then, amid the ruins of their dinner, he followed the instinct that had gripped him since the moment he'd met her, gathering her up in his arms and protectively holding her small, warm body against him.

She didn't protest, merely turned her cheek against his chest and relaxed into his hold as if she trusted him. Which of course she shouldn't. Because he was only taking care of her for his child's sake, naturally, not for any other reason.

And certainly not because he cared in any way about her.

Why would he? When he barely knew her?

Yet still the way she nestled in his arms made something in him want to growl with a possessive, primitive sort of satisfaction, a feeling he'd never had before and didn't particularly like.

Deciding it was probably another biological reaction, Dante ignored it, heading through the living area and into the bathroom.

Once there, he got rid of the remains of their clothing and turned on the shower, drawing Stella into the huge, white-tiled shower stall. There were about five different shower heads and he turned them all on, holding her as the hot water streamed over them.

She kept her head against his chest, her cheek pressed to his bare skin, her body relaxed against his. Her eyes stayed closed, her lashes spangled with drops of water, and the way she rested against him—

as if she was safe—made the possessive feeling inside him deepen still further.

A mistake.

He didn't want to possess her. He didn't want to possess anyone. He didn't want, full-stop. It was safer, less painful and far, far less complicated not to want anything at all.

He'd learned that lesson the day his mother had dragged him away from the brother he'd loved to a lonely, dangerous existence in the gutters of Naples. Where she'd ignored all his childish pleas to stop drinking, seeming to prefer the bottle and the company of the violent boyfriend she'd hooked up with.

Dante had tried to protect her when he'd finally got old enough to give that bastard a taste of his own medicine, only to have his mother scream at him for hurting poor Roberto and then threaten to report him to the police.

Anger that he thought he'd extinguished a long time ago flared into life, glowing sullenly in his gut.

In fact, he'd tried to protect her for years and she'd thrown it back in his face every single time. And then, when she'd got hurt, as she inevitably had, she'd ended up blaming him for it. The way she'd blamed him the night she'd died.

She was right, though. That was *your fault.*

He ignored the thought entirely, getting some shower gel from a bottle on the shelf and stroking it over Stella's skin, washing her gently. She relaxed totally against him, not saying anything, her breathing deep and slow. Almost as if she'd fallen asleep standing up.

No, he didn't want to think about his mother, not here, not now. In fact, what he wanted was to push Stella up against the tiled wall and forget his doubts by exploring her lovely body and making her scream his name again. But he wasn't going to. She was clearly exhausted and needed sleep more than anything else.

Dante finished washing her body then began to wash her hair, as it was clear that hadn't been done in a while. She didn't protest and didn't move, only giving a sensual little sigh as he massaged the shampoo through her scalp. The sound didn't help his aching groin, but he ignored that too, making her hair smooth and shiny with the conditioner before helping her out of the shower and drying her off.

'Why are you being so nice to me?' she murmured as he picked her up again, gathering her close as he carried her out of the bathroom.

'Because you're pregnant and you're tired and you need looking after.' He moved down the hallway and into the massive bedroom with its view out over the rooftops of Rome. Facing the view, pushed up against the opposite wall, was the huge bed piled high with soft bedding and white pillows—he liked to be comfortable.

'No, I don't,' Stella muttered sleepily as he pulled back the duvet and laid her down onto the bed.

'For the sake of the baby you do.' He pulled the covers around her, making sure she was comfortable, ignoring the urge to climb in beside her and hold her soft, naked body against his, protect her while she slept.

She was safe here, and anyway lying beside her would only make him hard, and he definitely didn't need any more temptation where she was concerned. He'd given in to it out there on the terrace, but he wouldn't again, not with the possessiveness he was already feeling.

Best not to make it any worse.

Dante turned away, only to have her reach out unexpectedly, her slender fingers wrapping around his and holding on.

He stilled and looked down at her. 'What is it?'

Her hair was spread like damp, golden silk all over the pillows, her eyes wide and dark. 'Where will you sleep?'

'The couch probably.' He hadn't thought about it, not that he was tired.

A strange expression crossed her face and then her fingers tightened around his. 'Don't…don't go.'

Surprise caught at him. 'Why?'

'I just…' She stopped, glancing away. But she didn't let go of his hand. 'I'm…cold.'

He didn't think she was and it made something pull tight in his chest, something he didn't want to examine too closely.

He should refuse. Turn around and walk out of the room. Yet he didn't.

Instead he gently tugged his hand free then pulled back the covers and climbed into bed beside her. She settled against him as he arranged her so her spine was to his chest, the soft curve of her bottom fitting against his groin.

He wasn't used to dismissing his body's physical wants, yet he found himself doing so now, ignoring how hard he was and how he ached, biting back a groan as she snuggled back against him, nudging the ridge of his erection.

Then she sighed and relaxed and he found he'd unconsciously spread his palm out on her bare stomach in a protective, possessive movement.

Because of the baby. Of course for the baby.

And yet it wasn't the baby he was thinking of as her breathing deepened and became more regular, her body soft, warm and yielding against him.

It was the feel of her fingers gripping his hand.

As if she was afraid to let him go.

Stella woke to find sunlight streaming across her face. She was lying tangled in a white sheet in the middle of a massive bed, and she was completely and utterly naked.

She was also alone.

Which was a mercy, given the memories of the night before streaming through her mind in glorious Technicolour. Dante taking her passionately on the table on the terrace. Dante staring down at her with fury in his eyes, demanding to know what she'd done to him. Dante gathering her up in his arms and taking her into the shower, washing her gently before putting her to bed.

Dante looking down at her with surprise as she'd grabbed his hand and begged him to stay…

A wave of humiliation swept through her and she rolled over, burying her face against the cool white cotton of the pillow.

She couldn't think what on earth had possessed her. That she'd let him wash her and put her to bed like a child was bad enough, but then to ask him to stay with her… Why had she done that?

It was true that after the two orgasms he'd given her she'd felt utterly exhausted, what little strength she'd had long gone. And when he'd gathered her up in his arms and held her against his hard, muscular chest she'd felt…safe and cared for.

It had been a strange, intoxicating feeling.

No one had taken care of her when she'd been young. Not her mother, who had been too busy running around after her brother, and not her father, who hadn't wanted to concern himself with a mere girl. Since her brother, as the heir, had always been more important, she hadn't questioned her parents' priorities. And, if she'd occasionally ached for someone to put their arms around her and tell her she was loved, well, that sensation soon passed if she ignored it.

Except she hadn't ignored it the way she should, had she? Because it had been that need for love that had been her weakness. Her flaw. It had got her brother captured, had broken her mother's heart and had turned her father even colder and harder than he had been already.

She thought she'd overcome that part of herself

years ago and she didn't understand what had made her surrender to Dante so completely the night before. What had made her relax against the heat and strength of his muscular body as he'd held her in his arms.

Perhaps it was the chemistry between them that had been the catalyst, blazing so brightly she'd been overwhelmed. Or maybe it was the discovery of her own power over him and the way she'd been able to strip that lazy playboy veneer away from him, exposing all the wild heat and hunger that lay beneath it.

Whatever it was, it couldn't happen again.

Stella closed her eyes, trying not to think about his fingers on her bare skin or how he'd felt inside her, moving hard and hot, holding her hands behind her back as he'd taken what he wanted from her...

No, most certainly it could not happen again.

'You're awake?'

She went still at the deep, rich sound of Dante's voice then rolled over and sat up, clutching the sheet around her, even though she knew it was pointless, considering he'd touched every inch of her when he'd washed her in the shower the night before.

He was leaning against the doorframe watching her, his hands pushed casually into the pockets of his expertly tailored dark-charcoal suit trousers, the look on his beautiful face guarded, leaving her with no idea what he was thinking.

'Yes,' she said coolly, drawing the sheet around her in a more decorous fashion. 'Obviously I'm awake.'

A fleeting ripple of amusement crossed his features. 'You don't fool me with that "ice queen" act, kitten. Not after last night.'

Heat rose in her face. 'Is there anything in particular that you want? I need to get dressed.'

They would not be having any discussions about last night, not if she could help it.

Dante's smile faded as quickly as it had come, the look in his eyes becoming oddly intent, and she was conscious of the tension crawling through her.

Whatever it was he was going to say it was obvious he was deadly serious about it.

'I've been thinking,' he said. 'About what to do.'

The tension began to wind like a clock spring, tighter and tighter. She swallowed. 'What to do about what?'

'I told you not to play games with me.' Gold glinted in his eyes. 'You know what I'm talking about.'

Stella tightened her grip on the sheet. 'The baby, you mean?'

'Yes, the baby.' He shifted against the door frame. Today he wore a dark-blue business shirt, open at the throat, exposing smooth, tanned skin and drawing her gaze to the strong, regular beat of his pulse.

Her mouth dried, her skin prickling all over with heat as she remembered what it had felt like to touch him, and how hot his chest had been when she'd laid her head against it listening to the beat of his heart.

'When our family was exiled from Monte Santa Maria,' he went on, as if he hadn't noticed her staring fixedly at his throat, 'we settled in Milan. However, as you know, my mother wasn't happy with our change in circumstances and, after a year or so, she decided to leave to find something better.' Dante's dark eyes gave nothing away. 'She took me with her, dragging me away from my home, away from what I knew and into a life where there was no stability and no protection. She was more interested in wine and violent men than in looking after me.' His tone was expressionless—too expressionless.

Very much against her will, Stella felt that same stir of curiosity that she'd felt the night before, when he'd related the facts of his life with the same dispassion as he did now. Which was wrong. Facts were fine—she knew them already anyway—but she didn't want to know anything beyond them.

He couldn't afford to become a person to her, not in any way.

'That sounds…appalling.' She wasn't sure what else to say. 'But how does this relate to the baby?'

Dante's gaze darkened, an odd intensity creeping into it. 'I've never done the right thing in my life. I've always avoided responsibility. But I cannot avoid it now. And I will not allow my child to be dragged into the sort of life I had.'

She blinked. 'You think that I would?'

'I don't know. Would you?'

Of course. He didn't trust her. As she already knew.

'No,' she said flatly, forcing away the sudden, hot lick of defensive anger, though why she should care what he thought of her one way or another she had no idea. 'I would not.'

'But I have no guarantee of that.' His voice was hard as iron, his gaze uncompromising. 'You have nowhere to go but that gutter I pulled you from yesterday or back to your parents in Monte Santa Maria. And, make no mistake, you will not be returning to either of those places.'

'I can—' she began hotly.

'Which leaves me with only one option.'

A formless, inexplicable dread began to creep through her. She hadn't thought about where she would go after her task was completed, because she hadn't allowed herself to think about it. And she didn't want to think about it now.

'And no doubt you're going to tell me what that is,' she snapped, angry that he was forcing this on her.

'Our child needs somewhere safe and stable to grow up,' he said steadily. 'And two parents to protect him or her.'

The dread pulled tighter. 'So what does that mean?'

'It means that you, kitten, will be staying here with me.' He paused, his gaze becoming even more intense. 'As my wife.'

Shock punched her hard in the gut and her brain blanked. 'Your wife?' she forced out, her voice hoarse. 'You cannot be serious.'

'I have never been more serious in my life.' There was nothing but darkness in his eyes now, every line of his handsome face set and hard. 'We will need to get married and then I intend to buy a family home where we will live together with our child.'

'But I—'

'It will be a marriage in name only,' he went on, ignoring her. 'I won't require anything from you physically. I'll find another outlet for my own needs.'

Stella fell silent, too shocked to speak, her brain struggling to catch up with what he was saying.

A marriage in name only. With the man she was supposed to revenge herself on. Creating a family with him and their child…

Her heart missed a beat, thundering loudly in her head, and for a second something hungry opened up inside her, a void she hadn't realised was there. Then she shoved the hunger away, before it settled too deeply, as another idea took its place.

This could be the opportunity she was looking for, a way to break him, to take the revenge that she needed for Matteo's sake.

He was famous for caring about nothing, except he cared about the baby. And he cared about giving that baby a home, a family. She couldn't bring herself to use their child to hurt him but…she could use herself, couldn't she?

Last night, on the terrace, she'd got a taste of her own power over him, the feminine power that was all hers. And she'd used it. So why couldn't she use it again? Why couldn't she use that to make him care about her the way he cared about the baby? Obviously, he had the ability to feel something, so there was the potential to make him feel something for her.

Make him fall for her, even.

Why would you think he'd fall for the woman who tried to murder him?

He might not. There were no guarantees. But this passion between them was too potent a weapon to ignore, and besides, what other option was there?

She had to try, at least. For Matteo's sake.

'You don't like that idea?' His voice came unexpectedly, almost making her jump.

Looking up, she found him watching her intently from the doorway.

'Wh-what idea?' she asked, struggling to remember what the conversation was about.

'A marriage in name only.'

'Oh, that.' She was pleased her voice sounded so level. 'That seems…fair.'

His gaze narrowed. 'Fair? I thought you might have more to say about it, quite frankly.'

Of course, he'd be expecting her to argue. And not to do so at least a little would seem suspicious.

You did so well with that last night.

Stella ignored the thought. Last night was last night. She could start by being conciliatory now. And, even though a marriage in name only obviously wasn't going to work, coming on too strong too soon would again arouse his suspicions.

'Is there any point saying anything?' she asked after a moment. 'You've obviously made up your mind. I would think I wouldn't get a say, correct?'

Dante's gaze sharpened. 'Do you want a say?'

'I suppose if a wedding is going to happen then I might want some input, plus I would like to help decide where we're going to live.'

He'd gone very still, watching her.

It made her nervous. Made her want to fuss around with the sheet to cover it.

'You're taking this very well,' he commented at last.

'Did you really expect me to fight?' She made herself meet his gaze, to show him she had nothing to hide. 'I don't have anywhere else to go, it's true, which means that staying here with you makes sense for the baby's sake. The marriage part of it seems extreme, however.' If she was going to put up a fight about anything to allay his suspicions, it needed to be that.

'It makes things easier from a legal standpoint and will also give the child some protection from your family.'

A little shock jolted her. 'My family?'

'They sent you to kill me, kitten,' he reminded her gently. 'Which means I do not want them anywhere near my child.'

She blinked. Of course. What was wrong with her? Her parents would no doubt have a reaction to her pregnancy and she knew already that it wouldn't be good. Her father would be appalled. He'd see it as an example of her weakness, her terrible flaw.

'I see,' she said blankly. She should probably protest that their child had nothing to fear from the Montefiores, but she couldn't say for certain that it didn't. Her father would do anything if he thought it would better their family.

'I'm sure you do.' Dante eyed her a second longer, then pushed himself away from the doorframe and straightened. 'You'll no doubt have some questions at some point. In the meantime, I'll be arranging a doctor's appointment for you.'

A doctor's appointment. A family home. Marriage...

The hungry black void inside her ached, sending a current of longing spiralling through her bloodstream. But she dismissed it.

All those things weren't going to happen. Because she was going to make Dante Cardinali fall for her. Care for her. And maybe let him think that she cared for him too. Then she would take all that away.

Perhaps starting that slowly was a mistake. Perhaps she should start making him fall for her sooner rather than later. Use the chemistry between them while it was still strong. Say...tonight, for example.

Dante's dark eyes scanned her face. 'You have something to say?'

'No.' Stella met his gaze, cold and hard and certain. 'Nothing.'

Yes, tonight. She'd start tonight.

CHAPTER SEVEN

DANTE SAT BACK on the big, white linen-covered couch and frowned at the laptop on the coffee table in front of him. He'd called one of his assistants that morning to send through a list of possible family properties, and he'd spent most of the day going through that list, viewing each one online to see whether any were worth visiting. There were a couple of likely looking candidates and he'd already got his assistant to make the arrangements for a viewing time.

He probably should have got Stella's thoughts on them but, now he'd decided what he wanted to do about the situation he'd found himself in, he wanted to move fast. With no half-measures either.

If he was going to claim his child and create the family he'd never had, then he was going to go all the way. He would marry Stella and buy a house where they would all live together as a family.

After all, it had worked for Enzo, so why wouldn't it work for him?

That way he could make sure his child had the best start in life, unlike himself.

He had thought Stella would baulk at the idea but, as he wasn't going to be moved on the decision, he'd decided to make it more palatable and less complicated by making it a marriage in name only. They didn't love each other and, besides, sex wasn't something he needed from her specifically; he could find physical satisfaction elsewhere.

She seemed in agreement, which in retrospect was odd, as challenging him appeared to be what she liked to do best. But he decided not to allow himself to think too deeply about it. Her agreement was all he required and she'd given it to him.

Of course, it had been a bit difficult to think about anything while she'd been sitting there draped in nothing but a sheet, looking all warm, sleepy and sexy.

Dante scowled at the laptop screen as his groin hardened, memories of the night before making him catch his breath.

Marriage in name only? Are you sure?

He forced the desire away. Of course he was sure. He could get sex anywhere. It didn't have to be with her. And certainly not, given how intense the sex had been between them. Because for this arrangement to work the focus had to be on the child, not each other. He didn't want…complications.

And if she wanted to get sex from somewhere else?

Then she could. As long as she was discreet, what did it matter to him?

Yet the thought made his jaw harden and tension coil inside him, the possessiveness he'd felt about her

the night before returning and sinking sharp claws
into him. And for some reason he couldn't stop thinking about the way she'd reached for his hand, her
fingers holding onto him, not wanting him to leave.
Almost as if she'd needed him…

His chest constricted, an insistence pulling at him,
and he had the horrible suspicion that in fact it would
matter to him if she got sex from somewhere else.
And that he would *not* like it one little bit.

There came a soft sound from one end of the room
and he lifted his head sharply to find Stella standing
in the doorway to the living area.

She had one of the plush, white towelling hotel
robes wrapped around her slight figure, her golden
hair cascading in a straight, gleaming fall of gold over
her shoulders, and there was a strangely hesitant look
on her lovely face.

He made a mental note to get one of his assistants
to look into getting some clothes for her, as she had
nothing but the jeans and ripped T-shirt that she'd
been wearing when he'd taken her from the apartment.

Her gaze met his, something he didn't recognise
moving in the depths of her blue eyes. A kind of agitation.

He hadn't seen her since that morning, having let
her have some space to process what he'd told her
while he'd got on with viewing houses and making
arrangements. But maybe that had been a mistake.
Was she having second thoughts?

'Good evening, kitten.' He pushed the laptop

closed and gave her his full attention, studying her face. 'Is there something wrong?'

'No, not at all. I just…wondered what was happening for dinner.' Her gaze flickered away from his before coming back again, as if she didn't want to hold it for long.

How odd.

'I see.' He put his hands on the couch in preparation for rising to his feet and going over to her. 'Then perhaps—'

'Oh no, don't get up,' she interrupted hurriedly, taking a few quick steps toward him. 'Is that the menu I see? I'll come and sit next to you.'

He stared at her in surprise as she closed the distance between them, sidling around the coffee table and sitting down beside him. She looked meaningfully at the menu sitting on top of the coffee table. 'Can I…have a look at that, please?'

She was very close, her thigh brushing his, and he was very aware that the white robe gaped at the neck, giving him a glimpse of bare, pink skin.

Underneath, she appeared to be naked.

Desire welled up inside him, thick and hot and demanding, and he suddenly wanted to pull the tie at her waist and uncover all those silky curves, bare her to his touch. She smelled of the shower gel he'd used the night before, a fresh scent, along with something feminine and musky that made his mouth water.

You really think you can do a marriage in name only?

Dio, he hadn't thought this would be difficult. He'd

thought that perhaps, after the night before, the desire would have faded. And it should have. So why had the simple act of her sitting close and wearing nothing but a robe got him so hard?

It shouldn't. He'd made a decision about his child. And that was more important than sex. He didn't need to sleep with her again so he wouldn't.

It was that simple.

Yet her blue gaze was very wide, looking up into his, and her lips were slightly parted in the most gorgeous, sexy little pout. The look on her face reminded him of that night in Monte Carlo, when she'd tried her hardest to seduce him.

Before he'd ended up drugged and handcuffed to the bed.

A premonition gripped him.

Her hand was in the pocket of her robe and he could see the tension in her arm. In fact, now that he looked, there was tension in her whole posture. Her entire body was vibrating with it and in the depths of her silver-blue eyes, behind the glow of desire, was that strange agitation again.

Except he knew what it was now.

Fear.

The tight thing in his chest clenched even tighter, though it wasn't with anger, not this time. 'Kitten,' he said quietly, staying quite still. 'I already told you. You're not going to kill me. You didn't do it back in Monte Carlo and you're not going to do it now.'

Stella's gaze flared silver with shock. 'What? I don't know—'

He didn't let her finish, instead reaching for the hand she had jammed into her pocket. She resisted, but he was stronger than she was, drawing her hand out despite how she pulled against him.

There was nothing in it. No knife. No gun.

She wasn't here to hurt him.

A sudden and intense relief gripped him, not for himself but for her. For the path that she clearly *hadn't* chosen. Because, while he'd always been certain that she'd never go through with hurting him, he hadn't been sure she wouldn't make another attempt.

There was pain in her eyes and she was breathing fast. 'You thought I was coming to kill you, didn't you?'

'I thought you might try.' He held her gaze so she could see the truth in his eyes. 'But I never thought you'd go through with it. I still don't.'

The narrow wrist he was holding began to tremble, but she didn't look away. 'So what would you have done if I'd actually had a knife?'

'Nothing.' He watched the fierce currents of her emotions shift over her delicate features. 'Because you wouldn't have done anything.'

'You don't know that.' Her voice was husky and threaded through with a very real pain. 'You expected that I would h-hurt you.'

He shouldn't care about this. He shouldn't care about her. Yet for some reason his assumption that she was here to make another attempt on his life had hurt her and he found he cared about that very much indeed.

You know she's not capable of it. But does she?

Dante stared into her eyes, noting the pain she couldn't quite hide and, beneath that, the fear.

It was clear that she'd come to him intending to do something but, as she didn't have a weapon, it wasn't to hurt him.

Except she was still afraid.

Was that because she thought she might? That she was afraid she *would have* gone through with it if she'd had a weapon?

He didn't like that thought. He didn't like that she was afraid, especially when she had no reason to be.

And there was only one way to prove it.

He let go her wrist, got up from the couch and went over to the large sideboard that stood against one wall, pulling open one of the drawers.

'Dante?' Stella sounded bewildered.

He didn't answer. Instead he picked up the long, sharp antique letter opener from the drawer and turned, coming back over to the couch with it.

She watched him, her quickened breathing audible in the quiet of the room, her gaze flaring as she saw what he was carrying. 'What are you doing?' she asked, her voice edged with alarm.

He ignored her. Sitting down next to her, he grabbed her wrist before she could move and slapped the letter opener into her palm. Then he curled her fingers around the handle.

Her gaze darkened as it met his and he could see fear stark in the depths. And his chest tightened, a deep sadness moving through him. Because the fact that she was afraid told its own story.

'Please,' she whispered. 'Don't…'

Without taking his gaze from hers, Dante slowly undid the buttons of his shirt and drew aside the fabric. Then he took her hand in his, guiding the point of the letter opener to his bare chest. 'My heart is here, kitten.'

Her breathing was fast in the silence of the room, the expression on her face stricken. The light flashed off the sharp blade of the letter opener as her hand shook. 'Why are you doing this?'

Reaching out, he stroked the silky, soft skin of her jaw. 'Because you're afraid. And I want to know why.'

She shuddered as he touched her, glancing down at the letter opener in her shaking hand. 'You shouldn't… trust me with this.'

'Do you want to tell me why not?'

'I might…hurt you.'

'No, you won't.' Gently, he followed the line of her jaw with his fingertips, using his touch to soothe her. 'You didn't back in Monte Carlo and you're not going to now. I wouldn't have given you a weapon if I thought you were even remotely capable.'

'But I was going to. That's what I came here to do now. Hurt you, I mean.'

His thumb touched her full lower lip very gently. 'How, kitten?'

A flush of colour flowed over her skin. 'I was going to seduce you. I was going to make you care for me, fall in love with me. And then I was going to leave.'

Part of him wanted to smile at the sheer naivety of that idea, but that would be unnecessarily cruel, and he wasn't a cruel man. And certainly not to a woman sitting there holding a blade to his heart, her eyes full of tears.

'That isn't possible,' he said. 'You can't make me do anything. And I'm famous for not caring about anyone. But what I am curious about is why you're so very determined to go through with this.'

'My brother—'

'No, I know about your family and why they wanted me dead. What I'm asking is why *you're* so set on taking any kind of revenge you can. Especially when it's obvious you don't actually want to.'

'I have to.' She was looking up at him, her expression full of that strange desperation. As if she was drowning and she was looking to him to save her. 'You don't understand.'

'Try me.'

'It's my fault.' She took a shaken breath. 'It's my fault Matteo died. I betrayed him. And so I owe it to my family and to his memory to go through with this. To be strong for once in my life and not...' She stopped abruptly, her voice cracking.

The tightness in Dante's chest constricted even further. 'Not what?' He cupped her cheek, her skin warm against his palm, encouraging her to go on.

Her throat convulsed as she swallowed. 'Weak.'

'Weak?' he echoed, frowning. 'Why would you think that?'

Her gaze glittered, more pain glowing in the depths. 'I told Papa I was strong enough to do this, that he shouldn't hire someone because it should be one of the family. It should be me, since I got Matteo captured. I promised him I wouldn't let him down again, but…'

The point of the letter opener moved and Dante felt the slightest nick of pain.

A horrified look flickered over Stella's face and she made a soft noise of distress, dropping the letter opener onto the floor as if it had burned her.

He looked down to see blood welling from the tiny cut she'd given him. 'It's just a scratch,' he said easily, ignoring the cut and reaching out to her.

But she jerked away, trembling all over. 'I can't do it,' she said hoarsely. 'I thought I could. But I can't. I can't do *any* of it.'

Dante caught her slender fingers in his. They were icy cold. 'Hush, kitten. Be still. It's okay.'

But she only looked at him, something naked and terribly vulnerable in her eyes. 'I should have had the strength to go through with it and I didn't. Papa was right. All along he was right. I'm weak, Dante. I'm nothing but flawed.'

Stella felt cold all over, as if she would never be warm again, and she was certain it was only Dante's large, warm hands holding hers that was keeping her from freezing to death right where she sat.

She knew she should pull away, try to recover what she could of yet another failure, but that void in her soul yawned wide and she couldn't seem to move.

It was true. It was all true. She was as weak as she'd always feared. As flawed as her father had always told her she was. She'd tried to be strong, to prove that she was equal to the task she'd taken on, to redeem her brother and assuage her guilt at her part in his capture. But, just as she hadn't been able to pull that trigger, she hadn't been able to cold-bloodedly seduce him either.

Instead she'd ended up telling him everything.

And all because she hadn't been able to stand the fact that he'd thought she was carrying a weapon and intended to hurt him with it.

That he'd been sure she'd never use it hadn't mattered.

He'd really thought she'd come to take his life again and there had been a very deep part of her that had found that terrifying. Because she couldn't blame him for thinking that. After all, she'd been the one to volunteer to kill him, no one else. Who was to say that if the opportunity presented itself she wouldn't do it?

Then he'd given her that opportunity. He'd held that blade to his own chest and invited her to do it, all the while stroking her gently, his dark eyes full of a terrible understanding that had undermined her in a way she'd never expected.

And all she'd been able to think about as she'd looked up into his beautiful face was him taking care of her the night before—washing her body and her hair so gently before tucking her into bed. Staying with her when she'd asked, wrapping her up in his powerful arms and holding her against his chest.

She never should have let him get under her skin the way she had, let the way he touched her and the things he'd said about his life matter to her. But somehow it had happened. And somehow he'd become more than the target he was supposed to be, more than the selfish playboy she'd only read about.

More than the vehicle of her own redemption.

He'd become a man. An actual person.

And she couldn't do it. Just as she hadn't been able to take his life back in that hotel room, she hadn't been able to stand the thought of hurting him at all.

Especially not when all her reasons for doing so were selfish ones.

Dante's hands tightened on hers. 'Not hurting a man doesn't make you weak,' he said forcefully. 'Who told you that nonsense?'

She couldn't tear her gaze away from the blood welling up on his skin where she'd nicked him. It made her feel sick, knowing she'd hurt him, even if it had been accidental.

Yet more evidence of her flaw.

'You're bleeding.' She tried to tug her hands from his, suddenly feeling frantic. 'I need to clean it. You might need stitches.'

His grip on her tightened, the look in his dark eyes intensifying. 'I'm fine. What I want to know is why you think you're weak.'

But there was a sick feeling in her gut, her own

heart beating hard in her chest like a bird trying to escape a cage, and she barely heard him. 'Please. The knife was sharp. It could have gone deep and then…'

Dante made an impatient sound. He let her go, shrugged out of his shirt, balled up the cotton in one hand then negligently wiped the blood away with it. The tiny cut began to clot almost instantly.

'There,' he said. 'Satisfied?'

But Stella couldn't stop from reaching out and putting one trembling hand on his hard chest near the cut, wanting to feel for herself that he was still warm. Still breathing. That his heart was still beating the way it should.

And it was. And he wasn't just warm, he was hot. Like a furnace. And there was so much strength beneath all that smooth, bronzed skin. So much power. So much intense, vibrant life.

How had she *ever* thought she could take that from him? Or that she could enact such a stupid, ridiculous substitute plan as making him fall in love with her?

She'd been naïve. So sure that she was as hard and as cold as she'd needed to be. Yet in the end all she'd been was selfish, thinking only of her own need for redemption.

She hadn't even thought about her baby.

Her eyes prickled, full of sudden tears, and she spread her palm out, pressing it hard against him, as if she could absorb that strength, take it for herself. As if the strength in him could heal the flaw in her, make her feel less selfish, less weak, less broken.

'Kitten,' he murmured. 'Talk to me.'

But she didn't want to talk, not right now, so she shook her head and bent, very gently kissing the cut she'd made instead. His skin burned against her lips, making her shiver, and she pressed her mouth to an unmarked part of his chest, wanting to taste him. Salty and hot and gloriously alive.

He went very still and then she felt his hand in her hair, stroking gently. 'I'm not sure that's a good idea.'

But she didn't want to be soothed or gentled. And she didn't want to be refused. 'Please,' she murmured hoarsely against his skin, desperation coiling inside her. 'I need you.'

His fingers tightened in her hair. 'Kitten…'

She ignored him, making her way up his chest to his throat, kissing him, tasting the powerful beat of his pulse. But it wasn't enough. She wanted more. She wanted his bare skin against hers, his heat melting the cold places inside herself, the places that had frozen the day her brother had been dragged away.

Dante's grip on her hair was too powerful to resist as he gently tugged her head up, the velvet darkness of his gaze meeting hers.

'Please, Dante.' She couldn't hide the desperation and didn't bother. 'I need this. I need *you.*'

And something in his expression shifted, gold glimmering in the inky depths of his eyes.

He didn't speak, yet her breath caught all the same as his grip on her changed and he drew her into his lap, urging her thighs on either side of his lean hips. Then he let go her hair, his hands at the tie of her robe, pulling it open, slipping it from her shoulders and off, baring her.

She reached for him as the fabric fell away, frantic for the touch of his skin on hers, and he responded, gathering her to him, and she gasped at the heat of his body. It was a glory, like the first touch of sun on a land ravaged by winter, and she arched against him, pressing the softness of her breasts to the hardness of his chest.

He made a rough sound, then his hands were on her and he was taking control, bringing them both down on the couch and turning so she was under him, and she moaned at the pleasure that stretched out inside her in response, loving his power and his heat. At how safe and protected she felt.

She lifted her hands and scratched them down his chest, feeling each hard, cut muscle, but then his mouth was on hers and his hips were between her thighs, and he was shoving his trousers down, getting rid of the fabric between them.

She gripped his shoulders, kissing him back feverishly, desperate and aching, need building higher and higher. But his kiss in return was slow and sweet, his hands moving on her gently, stroking, soothing her until she felt unexpected tears pricking the backs of her eyes.

Then his hands were beneath her, lifting her hips, and he was sliding into her, slow and deep, making her moan against his mouth. And he stopped there, deep inside, stroking her, his kisses becoming small nips and gentle licks, easing a part of her she hadn't realised was drawn so tight.

Then he began to move, slowly and carefully, as if she was precious. Her throat closed up and, no matter how hard she blinked, she couldn't make the tears go away. And she couldn't stop them as they slid down her cheeks.

She didn't want to cry, not in front of him. Not while he was deep inside her, the evidence of his strength and power outlined in every muscle, while she was weak and soft and so very broken.

But he didn't say a word, only kissed away the tears and held her tight beneath him, moving in a gentle rhythm that had her gasping his name as the pleasure began to build.

And then she wasn't crying any more, only staring up into his eyes, watching the gold bleed through the darkness until there was no darkness at all, only brilliant light.

Light inside her too, blinding her, a heat so intense it was going to burn her right here on the couch. And she wanted to burn. She wanted to blaze until there was nothing left of her.

She called his name as the fire became too bright to contain, too intense, pleasure flaming out of control. And he held her, kept her safe as she burned to ashes in his arms, before following her into the blaze himself.

Afterwards Stella didn't want to open her eyes. She wanted to lie for ever under Dante's powerful body and never move again. But she could feel him shifting as he drew out of her, the brush of his bare skin on hers making her shiver.

Was he leaving her here? She didn't think she could bear it if he did.

'You should call the police,' she said, trying for bravado. 'Get them to take me into custody. I did try to kill you a month ago, after all.'

'Don't be ridiculous,' Dante said. 'You're not going anywhere.' He sat up then slid his arms around her, gathering her into his lap so she was leaning against his chest, her head on his shoulder.

She didn't have the energy to make a fuss, so she didn't, content to sit there against his warmth, the afterglow of the orgasm, not to mention the aftermath of her own emotional breakdown, making her feel sleepy.

'Now.' Dante's voice was very firm. 'What you are going to do is talk to me. I want to know why you think your brother's death is your fault.'

Stella swallowed. She didn't want to talk about it. Then again, she did owe him some kind of explanation. 'It's a long story.'

Dante settled them both back against the couch. 'I have time and nowhere to be.'

His bare skin under her cheek was warm, his heartbeat strong and steady in her ear. It calmed her.

'My brother died in prison,' she said after a moment. 'He was stabbed in a brawl a few years after he was imprisoned.'

'Yes. I know. It read about it in your file.'

'What you don't know is that it was my fault he was in prison in the first place.'

'Oh? And why is that?'

It was painful to talk about this but she forced the words out. 'Papa and Matteo were plotting to get your father back his throne and the police got wind of it. Somehow Papa knew before they came and he and Matteo managed to get away. Only Mama and I were home and they…interrogated her.'

A shiver moved through her and she concentrated on the sound of Dante's heartbeat rather than the memory of her mother's sobs. 'She was fragile and the police weren't very nice. They made her cry. I was scared for her. Scared that they'd hurt her. Papa told me not to give the police anything, but I…couldn't be quiet. I'd seen Matteo go down to the caves near the beach near our house, so I…told them where he'd gone. So they would leave my mother alone.'

'Of course you did,' Dante said quietly. 'You wanted to protect her.'

He made it sound so reasonable, almost noble, when it was anything but.

'No.' Her voice had gone scratchy. 'It was wrong. Papa told me that I couldn't say a word to the police. He made me promise. He told me that Matteo was the most important person in our family and that he had to be protected. But…they were hurting my mother. And I was scared. And I thought that Matteo would get away—' She stopped abruptly, not wanting to voice it.

'But?' Dante asked after a moment.

The flaw inside her felt suddenly stark and jagged. 'I wanted them to love me. I wanted them to protect me. But they never did. They loved him more. And there was a part of me that wanted him…'

'Gone,' Dante finished with unaccustomed gentleness. 'Part of you wanted him gone.'

She closed her eyes again, unable to bear it, the guilt crushing. 'They took him and Papa was so angry with me. He knew why I'd betrayed my own brother—of course he knew. He told me I was weak, that if I'd truly wanted his love I would have done my duty to my family and not said a word.' Her throat closed and she had to force the rest of it out. 'And then Matteo died and Papa blamed me. He couldn't take it out on me, of course, so when he decided he'd take it out on the Cardinalis I volunteered to do the job.'

Dante reached for her discarded white robe, drawing it around her shoulders. 'Because you wanted to redeem yourself?'

'Yes. And because I wanted to prove to Papa that I was strong.' She tried to blink away the tears, shivering under the robe even though it was warm and Dante's bare chest even warmer. 'That I was worthy of his love.' A tear slid down her cheek. 'It's a flaw in me, Dante. And it caused my brother's death.'

But Dante's fingers were beneath her chin, tilting her head back, and she had no choice but to meet his dark eyes. There was something fierce and utterly sure in them. 'You didn't cause your brother's death, Stella Montefiore. It was his choice to plot against the government, not yours. The police wouldn't even have been after him if he hadn't and you wouldn't have been in that situation.'

'But—'

'And, as for wanting your father's love, that isn't a weakness or a flaw. That's a basic human necessity.' Something in his gaze shifted. 'My mother preferred the bottle to me, no matter how many times I tried to wean her away from it, so I understand what it's like to want something from someone who's never going to give it.'

She took a little breath. 'You didn't try to kill anyone for it, though.'

'No, I simply walked away.' There was a bitter note in his voice. 'And she died anyway.'

Stella stared at him, distracted for a second. 'What happened?'

But he shook his head. 'We're not talking about me. We're talking about you. And you're not flawed, Stella. You're not weak. It takes strength to push through with something you know is wrong, just as it takes strength *not* to do it too.'

'What do you mean?'

'I mean, you were very determined to carry out some kind of revenge.'

'And I couldn't.'

'No, you couldn't. But that's not a weakness. That was your strength. The strength to hold back when everything in you is telling you to do it.'

She wasn't sure he was right about that. But in this moment she couldn't find it in herself to argue. His dark eyes were very certain and there was a deep part of her that craved that certainty.

'You always knew I wouldn't,' she said, staring up him. 'Even back in Monte Carlo. Why?'

'I told you. I saw your soul that night. And it's not the soul of a killer.' His mouth curved very slightly. 'It's the soul of a lover.'

She couldn't stop looking at that mouth. Couldn't stop feeling the heat of the hard-muscled body beneath hers and the ache building between her thighs. An ache that was far more interesting to explore than talking. 'When you said that ours would be a marriage in name only…'

Dante's beautiful mouth curved more. 'Yes? What about it?'

She swallowed. 'Does that start now?'

'Well, seeing as how we're not married yet, no, it doesn't.'

'Good.' Stella reached up and slid her fingers into his thick, dark hair. 'Because you know what I really want?'

Gold flamed bright in his dark eyes. 'Tell me, kitten.'

'You,' she said thickly. 'I want you.'

And she drew his mouth down on hers.

CHAPTER EIGHT

DANTE SAT IN the waiting room of the high-end clinic he'd taken Stella to for her first doctor's appointment. The doctor had wanted a few minutes with Stella alone, which had made Dante want to protest for no good reason that he could see. But he'd held his peace and pretended he was absolutely fine with it.

He was not absolutely fine with it.

Restlessness coiled inside him, a feral sort of feeling that had grown deeper in the past couple of days. Oddly enough, ever since that incident with the letter opener.

He tried to tell himself it had nothing to do with how Stella had told him of her fears then reached for him as if he'd been the air she needed to breathe. Nothing to do with that at all.

Yes, he was continuing to sleep with her, but that was because she wanted it too, and why not? Work out this chemistry now, while they had a chance, because after the wedding that would be it.

Are you sure you want that?

Dante growled under his breath and shoved the

thought away. He shouldn't be concentrating on these ridiculous feelings anyway. What he should be concentrating on was the conversation they'd had about where they potentially might want to live.

By mutual unspoken agreement, they'd steered clear of personal subjects, keeping any discussions they did have firmly about the baby.

They'd agreed that since the child would be Italian they would need to live in Italy, but they'd had a minor argument about where. Stella had wanted a house in the countryside, while he'd preferred the city.

He'd shown her the list his assistant had given him and they'd eventually compromised by settling on a couple of places to view—one a *palazzo* uncomfortably near his brother's in Milan and a penthouse in Milan itself.

Dante thought he'd probably end up purchasing both anyway—he was going to need a place to himself, after all, especially to bring any potential lovers he might want to spend the night with—but he didn't want to have that discussion with Stella just yet.

The thought of sleeping with other women left him feeling unenthused and he wasn't sure what to do about it. He'd always planned to stick to his insistence that once they were married they would stop sleeping together, but celibacy wasn't an option for him either.

You could just keep on having sex with your wife.

His whole body tightened at that idea, yet there was something in him that also shied away from it. The sex was good—better than good, truth be told—but there was an intensity to it that made him uneasy.

Maybe because she's starting to matter to you?

Dante shifted in his seat then got up, unable to sit still any more, pacing around the waiting room.

Where the hell was that damn doctor?

His phone vibrated, thankfully distracting him from his thoughts. However, the thankful feelings drained away almost immediately when he saw a text from Enzo pop up on his screen:

Matilda told me you had a conversation with her about pregnancy. What's going on?

Dante sighed. *Dio*, what was he going to tell his brother? Enzo would no doubt find it extremely amusing that his playboy brother's past had finally caught up to him. Except that Enzo had no idea that the woman expecting Dante's baby had tried to kill him and was an enemy of the Cardinalis. And, if his brother ever found out, he'd probably have an aneurysm.

Which meant that until he had Stella safely as his wife Dante was better off not telling him anything at all.

He stared at his phone for a second then quickly typed in a response:

The usual private life drama. You don't want to know. It's not a problem now, anyway.

That should be enough for Enzo not to enquire further. He usually found Dante's preoccupation with the opposite sex quite dull.

Enzo, however, clearly had other thoughts.

It's not that 'romantic entanglement' is it?

Damn. Why couldn't his brother be uninterested, like he normally was?

Do you really want me to go into laborious detail? Dante texted back. *Or would you rather I work on that PR plan for the new office?*

There was a brief pause and then Enzo finally texted back:

Good point. Carry on.

It should have satisfied Dante that his brother—surprisingly for Enzo—had dropped the subject. But it didn't. It was almost as though Dante actually wanted to talk to Enzo about things child-related, which a couple of weeks ago Dante would have died rather than suffer through.

Things have changed.

Yes. As much as he wanted them not to, they had.

He was going to be a father and he wanted a different life for his child from the one he'd had. A life where his child would be safe, cared for and protected.

And loved.

A hot and painful feeling lanced through him, as though he'd been stabbed.

'You can come in now, Mr Cardinali.'

Dante ignored the sensation, grateful for the doctor's interruption.

Inside the doctor's office, Stella was lying on a special padded bed, dressed in a loose white hospital gown. She looked small and delicate and very pale, her golden hair in a cloud around her head. There was uncertainty in her blue eyes and, when they met his, he thought he saw a small flicker of fear that she quickly masked.

Understandable that she would be afraid. He wasn't exactly feeling calm himself, not when they were going to be getting the first glimpse of the child they'd created together and had no idea what to expect.

But he'd thought, after that night when she'd confessed to him and let him hold her as she'd cried, that she'd trust him at least a little with her fears, not try to hide them. Because she was going to have to trust him at some point, wasn't she?

He wanted her to. They were in this together, after all, and if they were going to be parents they had to trust one another. At least, they were if they were going to give their baby a better childhood than either of them had had.

Crossing the room to where she lay, he reached for her hand, ignoring the sudden surprised look that crossed her face as he did so.

Her fingers were cold so he enfolded them into his palm to warm them up.

Emotions he couldn't read flickered through her eyes and he could feel a degree of tension in her hand, though she didn't pull it away from his.

'You don't need to be scared,' he murmured when she didn't say anything.

'I'm not.' But she wouldn't quite meet his gaze.

'Don't try to hide it from me, kitten. You know I can see that you are.'

Colour stole through her pale cheeks. She kept her gaze averted, watching the doctor bustling around, remaining silent.

But her hand stayed enfolded in his, making the tight feeling in his chest deepen.

'Our baby will be fine,' he went on softly. 'I have you, kitten.'

She stared fixedly at the doctor, doing a good impression of ignoring him entirely. Then her fingers tightened around his, as if she found his presence reassuring, and the protective instinct inside him wound deep into his bones, making him ache.

She thought she was weak, yet she wasn't. She was strong. Yet even so, right now, right here, whether she acknowledged it or not, she needed him.

No one had needed him in a very long time, if anyone had ever needed him at all.

Mama certainly didn't, no matter what she said.

But now was not the time to be thinking of his mother, so he ignored the thought, keeping hold of Stella's hand as the doctor sat down beside the bed and prepared her for the scan.

The doctor talked soothingly about how everything was looking fine and there was no need for concern, and Dante wanted to tell her that he was not concerned at all, but the moment she put the wand on Stella's stomach his throat closed.

Then there was silence as the doctor shifted the wand around, all of them looking at the tiny screen on the ultrasound machine.

'Ah,' the doctor said at last, smiling. 'There is your baby.'

The sound of a heartbeat, fast and regular, filled the small room, and Dante found himself staring into the impossible silvery blue of Stella's eyes. She was looking straight at him this time, everything he'd been thinking himself reflected back in her gaze.

No, they hadn't looked for this. Hadn't wanted it. But it had happened, and now both of them would do anything and everything for the life they'd created between them.

'Give us a moment please, doctor,' Dante ordered, not letting go of Stella's hand or looking away from her.

'Of course.' The doctor rose to her feet. 'Take all the time you need.'

The door closed softly after her and then there was a long moment of silence as he and Stella stared at each other, the baby's heartbeat still echoing in Dante's head, Stella's small hand completely enfolded in his.

'I've decided something,' she said after a moment. 'If our child is a boy, I want him to be called Matteo. For my brother.' There was pain in her eyes, but a proud, strong determination was there too. 'Maybe his death wasn't my fault, yet I'd like to remember him all the same.'

Dante felt something in his chest shift, like sand under his feet, making him feel off-balance in some strange way. He couldn't tear his eyes away from her, feeling the words she'd said inexplicably resonating inside him. 'Yes,' he heard himself say. 'Matteo Cardinali. It has a good ring to it. And, if it's a girl, we can name her for your mother, perhaps?

Her eyes glittered and her grip on his hand tightened. 'What about you? Your family? Don't you have anyone you want to remember?'

His family. His terrible, dysfunctional family.

No, he had no one he wanted to remember, no one female anyway. There was only Sofia, his mother. His lovely, manipulative mother.

Why not her, though? It was a long time ago. You mourned her and then you moved on.

Naturally he'd moved on. But he did not want that tiny life to have her name, to be saddled with the weight of all that history.

Nothing to do with how angry you are at her?

No, he wasn't angry. Not any more. He'd washed his hands of her years ago and when she'd died… well…he'd grieved. But she was the one who'd chosen the path that she'd ended up taking. He'd tried to change her mind, to get her to stop drinking, stop seeing Roberto, but she'd ignored him. And then, on the eve of his sixteenth birthday, she'd told him that if he didn't like it he could leave.

So he had, thinking she'd come after him eventually. That she'd contact him, at least. That she wouldn't just…let him go.

Except that was exactly what she'd done. And the next time he'd seen her she'd been in hospital with a head injury that she'd never woken up from.

She didn't care about you. You've always known that.

The thick, hot anger he'd always tried to deny seemed to come out of nowhere, burning inside him like a flow of lava, but as always he forced it down, pretended that it didn't exist. Because anger meant that he cared, and he didn't. Not in the slightest.

If you truly didn't care, then it doesn't matter what you call your child.

'Dante?' Stella was sitting up now and he was conscious that she was holding him tightly, as if he was the one who needed reassurance.

Ridiculous. He was fine.

'There's no one in my family I want to remember. In fact, I would rather our child *not* have a name associated with that kind of history.' Gently but firmly he loosened her hold and rose to his feet because he wasn't going to have this discussion, not now. 'Get dressed. Time we went back to the hotel. I have a few properties I want to show you.' Then, without waiting for a response, he strode to the door and went through it.

Stella got out of the bath that Dante had run for her, drying herself off before pulling on the soft, blue silk robe he'd bought for her a couple of days ago and belting it tightly at the waist. Then she moved over to the doorway and went out into the living area of the suite.

Dante was sitting at the stone table on the terrace, concentrating fiercely on whatever was on the screen of his laptop. He'd been like that all afternoon since they'd returned from the doctor's office—working, apparently.

She'd found it all a bit overwhelming, the reality of seeing their baby's heartbeat on the ultrasound screen still resonating inside her, along with all the emotions that brought with it. Emotions she'd been trying very hard to deny since she'd first discovered her pregnancy, using her mission as an excuse not to think about it.

But, as she'd well and truly let go of that mission, she had no excuses now.

This was happening. She would be a mother.

It terrified her. She had no idea how she was going to do this, none at all, especially when her own parents hadn't exactly set her a good example. How did a woman who'd been determined to kill a man transform into a good mother? How could she do the right thing for a child when she'd been so set on doing the wrong thing for so long?

All she knew was that the moment Dante's dark eyes had found hers in the doctor's office she hadn't felt alone. She'd tried to hide how uncertain and scared she was, tried to hold onto the vestiges of her hard armour, but he'd seemed to see her fears anyway. Then he'd taken her hand, wrapping hers in his big, warm palm, and she'd felt that strength of his flow into her and all her fear and uncertainty had simply melted away. Almost as if nothing bad would happen now that he was here.

Stella leaned against the doorframe, studying the man on the terrace. He was in a plain white business shirt and dark-blue suit trousers, the sleeves of his shirt rolled up to expose the strong bones of his wrists and the long line of his muscled forearms. He had his elbows on the table, a line between his straight dark brows as he concentrated.

She was going to have to contemplate all the other bits and pieces of reality that she'd been avoiding, such as the fact that he intended to marry her and buy a house for them to live in together as a family.

An ache collected in her chest.

The past few days he'd been full of plans, showing her potential houses and talking about the kind of life they would build for their child together. She hadn't argued with any of it. Mainly because she had nowhere else to go.

She couldn't go back to Monte Santa Maria, not when her father was still expecting her to return triumphantly, the honour of the Montefiores safely intact.

He'd texted her requesting an update and she'd told him everything was going according to plan. She couldn't tell him the truth, not when she knew he'd only send someone else after Dante to do what she wasn't able to.

He'd discover that she had no intention of following through with his revenge plans eventually, of course, but she wanted to put that discovery off for as long as possible. To give her time to think about how to handle it.

Her only alternative to Dante's plan would be to insist on going her own way, find her own apartment and get a job, a task made even more difficult by the fact that her only work experience to date was waitressing. And then what would she do when her father found out she hadn't completed the task he'd set for her? And, worse, that she'd had Dante's child? He wouldn't welcome his grandchild with open arms, that was for sure.

No, marrying the billionaire and living in the house he'd bought for them, while he ensured their child got the very best of everything and kept them safe, was obviously going to be the best route forward.

The ache in her chest intensified, though she didn't really understand why, not when this outcome was the best for all of them.

You know why. He'll take care of you, but nothing more.

But she didn't want anything more, did she? Yet she could feel the pieces of that jagged flaw shifting around in her chest, the need for someone to put their arms around her, tell her that she was loved, still raw inside her.

Ah, but it didn't matter what she wanted. She was done with being selfish. The only thing that mattered was that their child would have the best start in life and right now that start was with Dante.

She him watched as he worked for a second longer, wondering at the journey he'd made in her head from being a target, to a media caricature, to a man. A warm, protective man. And yet somehow he'd still remained a mystery.

A mystery she wanted to know more about.

Did he really have no one from his family he wanted to remember? She hadn't asked him about his mother's name for their child, because he'd sounded so angry every time he'd talked about her. But there had to be someone else, surely?

His past was clearly a painful story, but he knew her guilty secret. About her brother's death and her role in it. So shouldn't she know at least a little about his? He would be her husband. They would be living together and bringing up their child. Shouldn't she know something of his family history?

Stella stepped out onto the terrace.

'How was your bath?' Dante asked, not looking up.

'Very nice. Thank you for running it for me.'

'No problem. By the way, I've organised a viewing of the *palazzo* in Milan for tomorrow. I'll get one of the helicopters to take us.'

'Okay.' She came over and leaned against the edge of the table and looked down. His face was set as he stared at the screen, the neck of his shirt open, and he wore no tie.

He was so incredibly attractive, so overwhelmingly beautiful.

Her mouth watered and she very much wanted to bend and kiss his throat, taste his skin.

How are you going to cope with this sexless marriage he's insisting on?

The thought arrowed through her, unexpectedly painful. Another thing she hadn't thought about because she'd assumed it wasn't going to happen. But it was going to happen. Regardless of how many nights she'd spent in his bed, he'd continue to insist that once they were married it would stop. That he wouldn't demand anything further from her physically and that he would find his satisfaction elsewhere.

She did not like that one bit.

But that was a discussion that would lead to uncomfortable places and she didn't want to have that conversation with him. Not now. First she was here to learn more about his family.

Her heartbeat sped up, her palms sweaty. 'I've been thinking about what you said in the doctor's office,' she said hesitantly. 'About not wanting to name our child after anyone in your family.'

His gaze remained on the screen. 'I haven't changed my mind, if that's what you're expecting.'

'I'm not. I just… What happened? With your family, I mean?'

'I told you. I was taken away by my alcoholic mother to live in Naples. She died years ago there.'

'How?'

Dante finally looked up at her, his expression guarded. 'Why do you want to know? It's not a very pleasant story.'

Very clearly, it was not, considering how obvious it was that he didn't want to tell her.

'My brother's story isn't very pleasant either,' she said. 'But I still told you.'

His gaze darkened. 'What is this? A quid pro quo? You tell me a secret and now I have to tell you one of mine?'

Stella didn't flinch. 'I'm going to marry you, Dante. Is it wrong to want to know something about the man who's going to be my husband?'

'It won't be a typical marriage, need I remind you?'

She ignored the slight, fleeting pain that pulled inside her at the words. 'I realise that. But I want to know more about you and your past. About what kind of father you're likely to be.'

A fierce, hot spark leapt to life in Dante's eyes. 'You think I would do anything to hurt our baby?' The question was soft but there was a whole world of threat in his deep, rich voice.

Stella refused to look away. 'No. And that's not what I was implying. Don't be so touchy.'

He made an impatient sound and, strangely, it was he who finally glanced away. 'You want to know what happened to me and my mother? Fine. She never quite recovered from my father losing his throne and so, when we were exiled from Monte Santa Maria to Milan, she started drinking. My father didn't care about anything but being king again, and he certainly didn't care about her. So after a couple of months she decided that she'd had enough. She left and took me with her.'

Bitterness laced his beautiful voice, like arsenic in hot chocolate. 'I didn't want to go. I'd already lost my country, and I didn't want to lose my family, and especially not my brother. But she didn't care what I wanted. All that mattered was that she wasn't alone. We ended up in some dirty tenement in Naples, surviving on nothing because she couldn't hold down a job.' He paused, gold gleaming hot in his eyes. 'You want to hear more or is that enough? It doesn't get any better, I warn you.'

She held his gaze, fascinated by that hot glow, the raw emotion he kept locked inside the darkness of his gaze like a candle flame in a dark room. It reminded her of the way he looked at her in bed sometimes when he thought she was asleep, as if she had something he wanted that he didn't know how to get.

'Yes, more,' she said. 'I can handle it.'

He let out a long breath, then closed the laptop and sat back on the seat. A smile was playing around his mouth, but there was no amusement in it. It looked forced. 'Of course you can. You were going to kill me, after all.'

There was a bite to the words that she was sure was supposed to hurt her, but she ignored it. He was angry because she was pushing him and he didn't want to be pushed. But too bad. Underneath anger there was always pain, as she knew all too well, and she wanted to understand it.

Why? So you can heal him?

The ache in her chest deepened. Well, why not? He'd helped her with the pain of her own guilt. Couldn't she help him in return?

No, she wasn't supposed to care about him. But somehow she did all the same.

'Perhaps I should have,' she said coolly. 'Apparently attempting to kill you is easier than getting you to talk.'

A flicker of emotion crossed his face, the gold in his eyes glowing hotter.

She wasn't surprised. If she'd learned anything about Dante Cardinali, it was that he preferred a fight to honest discussion. Which she had too—at least up until she'd seen her baby's heartbeat on that monitor.

He gave a low, mirthless laugh. 'You're a hard woman, kitten. You don't let me get away with anything do you?'

'Why should I? You didn't let me get away at all.'

His smile this time was more natural, and he got up, moving to where she leaned against the table and standing in front of her. Then he settled his hands on her hips and lifted her onto the table top, pushing himself between her thighs and fitting her against him. He was hard, the heat of him seeping through the fabric of their clothing, and she shivered, loving the delicious press of him against her. But she didn't look away, keeping her gaze on his.

Dante shook his head. 'You're not going to let this go, are you?'

'No.'

'Okay. So, we moved around Naples a lot,' he went on, his tone casual, stripping the words of any emotion. 'Since my mother couldn't stay in any one job too long, it meant she couldn't pay rent. Eventually she took up with a series of men who would help her out sometimes. Her favourite was a bastard called Roberto, who beat her when he was drunk. But for some reason she loved him and when I finally grew big enough to put a stop to him taking out his moods on her—and sometimes on me as well—she blamed me for hurting him. And for us subsequently moving again, because Roberto stopped the money he was giving her.'

Stella's heart squeezed. He sounded as if he'd told this story a hundred times and was bored of it. But she could hear the tension in his voice, an undercurrent of anger and of pain. It made her want to do something for him, but she wasn't sure what, so she put her hands his forearms, her fingers on his bare skin, hoping the contact would give him some comfort.

'I tried to make her stop drinking,' Dante went on, his voice becoming harder and more edged. 'Tried to get her to leave Roberto. I did everything I could think of, telling her that it would kill her if she went on like she was, but she wasn't interested in stopping, or changing what she was doing. So in the end I gave her an ultimatum—told her it was either the bottle or me. I was just sixteen, old enough to look after myself—though, to be frank, I'd been doing that since she dragged me away from Milan—so when she said that she wasn't going to stop, that I should go if I couldn't handle it, that's exactly what I did.'

He smiled, sharp and white. 'I walked out, thinking she'd come after me. That she'd change her mind. But she didn't. For six months I heard nothing and then I got a call from a hospital saying that she was in Intensive Care with a head injury. She'd fallen over after a night drinking with Roberto and had hit her head on the pavement.' A muscle ticked in his jaw. 'I spent a month sitting beside her, watching her slowly die. She never regained consciousness and so she never knew that I'd come back.'

The anger in his gaze gleamed, his fingers gripping her tighter, though she didn't think he was aware of it. 'I never got to ask her why she'd dragged me around Italy with her, since it was obvious she preferred the bottle to me. Or why she wouldn't stop drinking, even when I begged her to. She just died and left me with nothing. Just like she always did.'

Stella swallowed, grief closing her throat. For Dante and the pain that was obviously still raw inside him. 'Dante,' she said thickly, not sure what else to say or what else to offer. Her own parents hadn't left her with anything either.

His mouth twisted in another of those terrible smiles. 'So now you know exactly what kind of man you're marrying, kitten. Stateless. Rootless. A man who'd rather walk away from a problem than have to deal with it, because it's easier to not give a damn.'

Of course. The 'problem' he'd walked away from had been his mother.

'You blame yourself,' she said, before she could think better of it. 'Don't you?'

'What? For the way she died? No, of course not.' Dull anger glittered in his eyes. 'She chose that path herself. I had nothing to do with it.'

'If you truly believe that, then why are you so angry about it?'

'Angry? I'm not angry.' He laughed, but there was no amusement in the sound. 'That would imply that I care. And I don't. Not any more.'

But he was lying, that was obvious. Of course he cared. He cared deeply and she could see the depth of it in the pain that lay underneath all that anger.

'Yes, you do.' She lifted her hand and touched the

warmth of his cheek. 'And that's the problem, isn't it? You care too much.'

The smile on his face vanished. 'Is there a point to this?' His hands firmed on her, his hips flexing slightly, the ridge of his erection nudging against the soft, sensitive place between her thighs. 'Because there are things I'd rather be doing.'

Stella fought back the shiver of pleasure that whispered over her skin. It would be easy to surrender, to let him distract her in the way he was so good at, and part of her wanted to. She wouldn't have this for ever, after all.

But this was important.

'The point is that you're angry,' she said quietly, looking straight up into his eyes. 'And I want to help you the way you helped me.'

His mouth twisted. 'Don't care about me, kitten. That would be a mistake.'

'And is that what you'll say to your child when they tell you that they love you? That it's a mistake? That they shouldn't?'

It was a low blow and she knew it. But, whether he liked it or not, this mattered. For the baby's sake if nothing else.

His gaze went dark, any flickers of gold vanishing from it entirely. 'Don't use our child to manipulate me,' he said, low and hard. 'I won't allow it.'

Stella stared back. 'I'm not. I don't care what you feel for me, but I need to know that you'll care for our child.'

Liar. You care what he feels for you.

She ignored the thought, meeting Dante's black gaze head-on, keeping her fingers pressed to his cheek, letting her know how serious she was.

'Do you really think I wouldn't?' he demanded roughly. 'Why do you think I offered to marry you? Why do you think I'm buying a house for us to live in?'

'You're doing those things to take care of us, Dante. But that is not the same as love and you know it.'

'Love?' The word was a sneer, sharp-edged and painful. 'Since when does love have anything to do with it?'

Her heart gave one hard beat in her chest. She refused to look away. 'Since now.'

Stella's fingertips on his skin were light, her body against his soft and warm, and he felt as if he was holding a sunbeam in his hands; all he wanted to do was bask in her heat.

He most certainly didn't want to look into the relentless silver-blue of her eyes and talk about the farce that was love. He'd already given her more of himself than he'd wanted, more than he'd given anyone in his entire life, including his brother.

And he wasn't sure why. He'd never felt obligated to be honest with another person simply because they'd been honest with him. In fact, he'd tried never to feel obligated to anyone at all. He didn't want to give any more pieces of his soul away than he had already.

He'd been in a foul mood since they'd got back from the doctor's office and when she'd brought up his family his temper had become even fouler.

Nevertheless, there had been something direct and honest in her gaze that he hadn't been able to refuse. That had made him want to give her something in return for what she'd given him: her secrets and her pain the night he'd made her hold a blade to his chest. The way she'd clutched onto his hand as they'd seen their baby on the monitor. Her pleasure, every time he touched her at night.

Those had all meant something to him, especially when his mother hadn't wanted anything at all from him. She'd ignored what he'd tried to do for her, had thrown all his offers to help her back in his face. And when he'd attempted to help anyway she'd told him that he didn't care. That, if he truly loved her, he'd leave her alone.

Even in dying she'd refused him.

But Stella hadn't. She'd accepted his help, let him take care of her. Let him give her strength and hold her. Stella had never refused him anything. Which meant he hadn't been able to refuse telling her about the life he'd had with his mother. But he'd hoped that, once he'd finished, she'd leave the subject alone.

Apparently not.

'What is it exactly that you're asking?' he demanded, trying to sound like his normal, casual self and knowing he'd failed. 'Because, if you're wanting me to fall on my knees and tell you that I'm madly in love with you, you're going to be disappointed.'

'I know that,' she said without a flicker, full of a quiet dignity that made an inexplicable sense of shame creep through him. 'I'm not talking about me. I'm talking about our child.'

Anger burned sullenly inside him, a dull flame that never seemed to go out no matter how many times he tried to ignore it.

He didn't want to talk about love. He didn't even want to think about it.

Love was his mother throwing a glass at his head when he'd tried to call a doctor for her after a hard night on the tiles. Love was her threatening him with the police after he'd punched Roberto in the face after the bastard had hurt her.

Love was her telling him that she was done with him and he should leave her alone.

Love was her dying in that hospital bed without ever regaining consciousness, denying him his last opportunity to talk to her.

He'd been there, done that and he wanted no part of it ever again.

'Our child will have everything in my power to give,' Dante said, trying to dismiss the subject. 'Call it what you want.'

Yet there was something in Stella's gaze that felt like a hand closing around his heart. 'And if he or she wants to love you?'

The hand squeezed harder. 'I won't stop them.'

'But you won't give them anything back?'

The words twisted inside him like a barb on a fishhook, tearing and painful. 'Do I need to?' He squeezed her gently, flexing his hips, sliding his erection against the softness between her thighs, the delicious ache easing the agony of his memories. 'When they'll get all the love they might want from you?'

Stella's gaze darkened. Gilt curls still damp from her bath stuck to her forehead. She smelled of lavender and musk, and he wanted to bury his face between her breasts, breathe her in. Then maybe lick a long path down between her thighs too, make her scream instead of asking him questions he didn't want to answer, or make him talk about things that should have been left in the past.

Things such as the knowledge that maybe, if he hadn't walked away from his mother, he might have been able to save her.

That she wouldn't have died the way she had.

Because it's your fault. It's always been your fault.

'You don't mean that,' Stella said.

'How would you know? You don't know a thing about me.'

'Wrong.' Her fingertips moved lightly along his cheekbone. 'I know that you care about this baby, whether you like it or not. And I know you want to do the right thing by it.' Her touch moved to his jaw. Why he was letting her touch him like this he didn't have any idea, but he didn't stop her. 'I know you've done nothing but look after me since you brought me here, despite the fact that I wanted to kill you. And I know you're angry. You're very, *very* angry about your mother and, Dante...' She touched his mouth gently, meeting his gaze. 'You have a right to be angry. You needed her and she wasn't there for you, and there is no excuse for that. None at all.'

Tension crawled through him, tugging at his instinct to pull away violently, to turn and leave, no matter how that would hurt her.

But he couldn't do that.

Colour had risen in her skin, making her eyes look bluer. A perfect, pale white-and-gold china shepherdess of a woman. Not a woman he'd ever have picked to hold a gun to his head or end up carrying his child. Not a woman he'd have picked to fight him, challenge him on just about every level there was. Yet she'd done all of those things.

A vulnerable woman too—he couldn't forget that. One who'd been hurt by her past, and whose feelings had been twisted and denied, yet despite that she still had an open heart. She wasn't like him. She would never *not* care.

Which made her the most perfect parent for their child.

Unlike you.

But he didn't want to think about that, still less talk about it. He was done with anger and guilt. He was done with caring. And he was done with love.

Especially now he had Stella, warm and lush and naked under that thin blue silk robe.

'I think we've done the topic of me to death.' He flexed his hips again, pressing himself against her damp heat. 'I'm more interested in other things.'

Her fingers gripped his forearms tightly, the expression on her face making that fist around his heart squeeze like a vice. 'You can trust me, Dante. I know that sounds strange, coming from the person who held you at gunpoint a month or so ago, but you can. I will never turn you away.'

The tight, painful feeling in his chest grew stronger and he had to grit his teeth against it. 'I don't want your trust,' he growled, knowing he was being a bastard and not caring, because not caring was supposed to be what he did. 'What I want is your body, understand?'

'Yes.' Her gaze was too sharp, too knowing. 'And you can have it. I told you I will never refuse you and I meant it.'

She wasn't supposed to do that. She wasn't supposed just to…give in to him.

His heart rate began to climb, adrenaline pouring through him. 'Bad idea, kitten.' His voice was low and much rougher than he'd intended. 'I'm not in a gentle mood.'

'I don't care. Do your worst. I'm stronger than I look, remember?'

Oh, yes, he remembered.

He lifted her into his arms, because he wasn't going to take her on the stone table like an animal, not again. He could at least be an animal in the comfort of the bedroom where there was something soft to ravage her on.

Bending his head, he took her mouth in a hard kiss, letting her know that he most certainly would take whatever he wanted from her. But she only wrapped her legs around his waist and gripped him tightly, opening her mouth, letting him kiss her harder, deeper. Showing him the truth—that she would never turn him away. Never refuse him. She challenged him and pushed him, gave him the fight that he wanted, and then she opened her arms and took him in, giving him the surrender he craved.

His heartbeat was wild and out of control, the familiar, intense desperation winding around his soul. He didn't know why it was like this with her every time. He couldn't understand it. But he couldn't stop the feeling that was rising inside him, a desperation, a need. To get close to her, have her warmth and softness all over him, under him.

The feeling pushed at him, battered against his heart, and he couldn't wait, not even to get to the bedroom. He stopped in the living area and laid her down on the thick, white carpet that wasn't as soft as he wanted it to be, but her scent and her heat were affecting him so badly that he just couldn't stop.

Pulling open her robe, he exposed her naked body to the late-afternoon sunlight pouring through the window. She was all golden hair and creamy white skin and soft shell-pink nipples. Her gaze was jewel-bright as she looked up at him, full of desire and need. Need for him.

'You want me?' he heard himself growl as he knelt between her thighs and leaned over her, putting his hands on the floor on either side of her head. 'You want me, Stella Montefiore?'

'Yes.' Her chest rose and fell, fast and hard in time with her quickened breathing. 'I do. So much.'

'And only me.' He didn't know why he was demanding this from her, especially when he was still intending their marriage to be a sexless one. But that didn't change the roaring need inside him, the hunger for something he didn't understand. Something only she, with her pride and stubborn determination, with her warmth and her surrender, could give him.

You can't go anywhere else for this. And you don't want her to either.

No. He damn well didn't.

'I've changed my mind,' he said roughly, deciding right there and then. 'Once we're married, you're mine. There will be no one else for you, understand me?'

Her hands came up, her fingers threading through his hair, her eyes blazing into his. 'Yes, I understand. And there will be no one else for you either.'

He almost laughed, because of course she would demand the same thing from him. Not that he was going to argue.

'I don't need anyone else.' He let her see the truth in his gaze. 'Not when you can give me everything I need.'

A fleeting brightness moved through her face, then she was tugging his head down, her lips meeting his, hungry and wanton.

And he was kissing her, a desperate, hot kiss, the heat of her mouth lighting a fire inside him that he didn't think would ever go out.

That should have been a warning, but he was too far gone to notice. He kissed her, taking what he wanted from her, feverish and desperate, tracking kisses down her neck before lingering in the soft hollow of her throat, tasting her frantic pulse. He wanted to spend more time tasting her, making her even hotter for him, even more desperate, but he couldn't wait. He'd never been able to wait, not with her.

He clawed open his trousers and spread her thighs, pushed himself deep inside her. She gave a soft cry of delight, lifting her hips to meet his thrusts, and he stared down into her face, into those shattered sky eyes, unable to look away. Her body was slick around him, her inner muscles gripping him as tightly as her thighs around his waist. As if she wanted to hold him close and never let him go.

And he shouldn't want her to. He shouldn't like it. It shouldn't feel as if he was somehow home.

But it did. And the feeling didn't go away as the pleasure inside him began to get more intense, more demanding. As he watched the same pleasure rise in her too.

So he eased back on his thrusts, pushing into her in a long, lazy glide then sliding out. Deep and slow. As if there was nothing better to do but this. As if he could do it all day. And he wanted to. He wanted it not to end.

Time slowed down to a pinpoint, to this one eternal moment. To her lying beneath him, her hips moving with his, her fingers twined in his hair, her gaze locked with his. Full of desire, full of need.

For him. Just for him.

'You're amazing,' she whispered, her brilliant gaze on his. 'You're the most amazing man I've ever met.'

It felt like an arrow to the chest, the pain bitter-sweet and intense.

Because right now, in her arms, for the first time in his life, he felt like he could possibly be that man. The man she thought was amazing instead of the man who'd walked away from a woman he was supposed to be there for. A man who'd let his own mother die, who'd wasted his entire life trying to drown in his own self-loathing, telling himself that he didn't care, not about anything.

But Stella was right, and that was the problem. He did care. He cared about *everything*.

And he thought he probably cared about her most of all.

'Dante,' she murmured, her hands twisting tighter in his hair. 'Take me home.'

So he did, reaching down between them, stroking the sensitive place between her thighs as he thrust, watching her eyes turn pure silver as the climax exploded through her.

Crushing his own cry of release against the softness of her mouth.

Knowing that, one way or another, he was going to end up hurting her.

And trying to tell himself it didn't matter.

CHAPTER NINE

STELLA GAZED AT the magnificent view out of the long, elegant windows of the *palazzo*, over rolling green lawns and terraced gardens surrounding a lavishly tiled pool area, to the small wood that lay beyond all that green.

It was so very beautiful. The perfect family home.

She and Dante were viewing the property he'd chosen near Milan, an old *palazzo* near his brother's, though Enzo and his family spent most of their time on the little island Enzo had bought the year before.

Stella had wanted to know more about Enzo—important, considering the man was going to be uncle to their child—but Dante hadn't been interested in telling her much about him.

In fact, since that evening on the terrace at the hotel in Rome, he hadn't seemed interested in talking to her much at all. It had been at least a week since then and he'd spent the majority of it at his computer or on the phone, organising various things. He was having to deal with a few issues with his business interests—or at least that was what he'd told her—as well as preparations for their wedding.

He'd told her he wanted her input on aspects of it, but she found that sitting down and talking about it made her feel…uneasy. All this talk of love and the importance of vows when both of them knew it wouldn't be a marriage based on anything more than shared parentage. It made her ache. For herself and for their child. For the kind of life that they would have, which sounded so very wonderful on paper, and yet…

Stella stared sightlessly at the lawns that stretched into the distance beyond the windows, trying to ignore the bleakness that gathered inside her.

Dante cared, she knew he did, but he wasn't going to admit it. And she couldn't force him to if he didn't want to. So what would that mean for their baby? What would it mean for their child to grow up with a father who wouldn't admit to the possibility of love?

She'd grown up without that in her life and it was her need for it that had propelled her to pick up the gun and point it at Dante's face. Her weakness, her fatal flaw. She would do everything in her own power to make sure her son or daughter grew up knowing they were loved, but would the love of one parent be enough?

Dante's was a magnetic, charismatic presence. He would have a massive influence on their child, especially given how involved he wanted to be in their life. But how would that child feel to have a father who never told them he loved them?

Pain echoed inside her, a vibration that shuddered

through her, reflecting off the empty places in her soul and reverberating like an echo.

She knew how that felt. Never to have someone hold her or tell her that they loved her. That they were proud of her.

It hurt. It hurt so much.

A footstep echoed in the empty room, and then warm arms slid around her waist, drawing her in close to the hot, hard strength of the man behind her.

She should have felt comforted and reassured by those arms, by the power in that body. But right now it didn't feel enough. Like a perfect fantasy that only half came true, the rest of it out of reach for ever.

Her child would feel like that. Wanting something from its father he was never going to give it. Oh, Dante might, at some point, admit to himself what his refusal to deal with his past was doing to him and to their child—because it was definitely his past that was holding him back.

Or he might not. He might never admit it.

You will have to hope that your love alone will be enough for your baby. Because what other option do you have?

She could leave. That was another option. But then where would she go? How would she provide for their child? And would Dante even let her? He wouldn't. Of course he wouldn't.

Can you *walk away from* him? *That's the real question.*

The thought sat inside her, a cold, hard reality she'd been trying to ignore for days now.

'What do you think?' Dante murmured, nuzzling against her ear. 'Do you like it?'

He was talking about the *palazzo*, of course, but she liked his arms around her, the feeling of his strength at her back, the warmth of his breath against her skin.

He'd changed his mind about marriage in name only. He'd told her that she was his and that they would find physical satisfaction with each other, and every night he proved it to her over and over.

But her doubts weren't about him and whether a playboy would ever be faithful—she knew he would be. He was a man of determination and he'd promised her that if she wouldn't get satisfaction elsewhere then neither would he. She believed he meant it.

No, her doubts were about herself. Whether sex would be enough of a stand-in for the hunger that lay in her soul. Whether a child would fill up that need and whether it was fair to expect a child to do that.

'I do like it,' she said, staring out the windows, conscious of the warmth of the man at her back and the hunger inside her that would go unsatisfied for ever. 'Perhaps it would be good to be close to your brother. Our little one will have a cousin to play with.'

He made a noncommittal sound. 'I'm not sure whether being close to Enzo would be a good thing or not. If you think I'm controlling, you haven't met him.'

'And will I?' She put her hands over his where they rested on her stomach, trying to ignore the doubts. 'Meet him, I mean?'

'You will. At our engagement party.'

Of course. Dante had made sure not a breath of what was happening between them made it into the media. He hadn't wanted anyone to know, or at least not until he was ready. Luckily it had only been a week, so no one had noticed his absence from the entertainment circuit.

She didn't much care about the media—wouldn't a press release do the job? But he'd told her to let him handle it his way. He'd decided on an engagement party as the best way to announce their circumstances, as the media tended to be less intrusive when they thought they were being given the whole story rather than a carefully selected portion of it. He'd made the observation that it would allow news of what was happening between them to reach her family, so she wouldn't have to deal with them.

She appreciated that. She'd told him about her worries concerning her father and what he might do once he'd found out she wasn't going through with his revenge plans. Dante's response had been to send a couple of his representatives to Monte Santa Maria to inform her parents that she was now under his protection, as she would be marrying him. He'd also included a payment of a ridiculous sum of money to keep Santo quiet, plus a warning that if he tried to contact Stella again the police would be called and he would be taken into custody.

Stella was fine with that. She didn't want to hear from her father. She'd made peace with Matteo's memory as much as she could and with her own failure to go through with her father's vendetta.

Except that weakness, that need for love, is still there.

'You are going to invite him, aren't you?' She kept her tone neutral, hiding the doubt that tugged at her.

'Of course I will. He's my brother.' Dante nuzzled her neck, pressing a kiss below her ear and making her shiver deliciously. 'Except we might keep the fact that we met while you were trying to kill me to ourselves for a while, hmm? Enzo's very protective.'

And so was Dante—she knew that for a fact.

'Are you afraid he'll do something to me?' she asked, curious.

Dante gave a low laugh. 'No. He'd be dead before he hit the floor if he tried to hurt you.'

Stella thought he was probably only a little serious. 'So why not just tell him?'

'He'll be angry and we really don't want an angry Enzo. We need to build up to that.'

Her heart ached at the affectionate warmth in Dante's voice. Yet another reminder that, despite what he'd told her, he cared. He cared about his brother, for example, and quite deeply. Why else would he have chosen to look at this *palazzo*—the one near Enzo's?

But he won't ever care about you.

Emotion clogged her throat. She didn't need him to care about her, though, did she? He was going to give her everything else: a place to live, financial support, help in bringing up their child and all the physical pleasure she might want. Did she really need him to care about her too?

You know the answer to that question.

Yes. She did. That was all she'd wanted all her life: someone to care about her. Someone she mattered to. But her parents had only ever wanted Matteo, not her. No one had ever really wanted her.

And now she was going to tie herself for life to a man who didn't really want her either.

Restlessness filled her and suddenly she didn't want to stand there with the warmth of his arms around her like the promise of something she was never going to get. She pushed his hands away and stepped out of his arms, moving over to the window and looking out.

Her heart thumped painfully in her ears and she felt oddly cold.

A silence fell, though she could feel the pressure of Dante's gaze from behind her.

'Kitten?' he asked after a moment. 'Is there something wrong? Something to do with my brother?'

'You care about him.' Stella turned from the view and looked at the man she was supposed to marry. 'Don't you?'

Dante stood there in one of his expensively tailored suits—no jacket today, and no tie either, his black shirt casually open at the neck, his sleeves rolled to his elbows. Her favourite look on him.

He had his hands in the pockets of his trousers and the look on his handsome face was guarded. 'He's my brother,' he said, frowning, as if that was all the explanation required. 'Why do you ask?'

Stella swallowed, not quite sure herself why she was asking. It was just…she couldn't stop thinking about his refusal to acknowledge the fact that he did care. About quite a lot of things. Was it only her he denied that to? Did he ever say that to his brother too?

'So you can care about people, Dante.'

'If you're wanting—'

'Will you ever care about me?' The words slipped from her before she could stop them and she knew she shouldn't have asked as soon as they were out.

But she couldn't take them back even though, as his expression hardened the way it had back on the terrace in Rome, the darkness of his eyes becoming absolute, she desperately wished she could.

It was a door shutting in her face.

No, he wouldn't care about her.

But you want him to.

The realisation opening up inside her was like a sunflower blooming, shining in her heart, bright and beautiful and golden, reflecting glory everywhere.

She'd always wanted someone to care for her, wanted an acknowledgement that she mattered to somebody. But she hadn't known she'd wanted that acknowledgement from Dante. No one else. Just him.

Dante, who wasn't the irresponsible playboy she'd first assumed, but who was warm and caring and protective. Who'd taken care of her, no matter that she'd tried to kill him. Who'd challenged her and pushed her. Who'd held her when she'd been vulnerable and broken, and who'd given her strength when she'd needed it. Not to mention the indescribable pleasure he also gave her every night.

Dante, who didn't want to care, not about anyone.

The sunflower began to wither inside her, its golden brightness fading as cold whispered through her, the icy breath of winter.

'It's okay,' she said suddenly, before he could speak, because she didn't want to hear him say the words out loud. She didn't think she could bear it. 'Forget I said anything.'

But he didn't look away and the set expression on his face didn't fade. His gaze was dark, his beautiful mouth hard, tension gathered in every line of his powerful body. 'Then why did you ask?'

He was angry with her, of course, and why wouldn't he be? They were here to view a house, not have a deep and meaningful discussion about their relationship.

Stella glanced out of the window again, not wanting to meet the anger in his gaze, wishing she'd never said anything. 'It doesn't matter.'

'It's about what I said to you in Rome, isn't it?'

'I don't need you to—'

'Because if you want the truth then here it is. I will care for you, Stella.' His voice was nothing but cold, hard steel. 'But, no. I can never care about you.'

The words felt like stones thrown at her, each one jagged and sharp, leaving a bruise where they landed. And the fact that they were the truth only made the pain worse.

Did you really expect anything different? He told you not to care about him.

He had. Yet she cared anyway.

No, it was more than that, wasn't it? More than simple caring.

She loved him. Because that glory inside her, the warmth, the brightness she felt whenever she looked at him, was love. The pain she experienced herself whenever he hurt, that was love too. The longing to touch him, have his arms around her, have him be the one to fill the void inside her...

What else could it be?

Only love.

Nothing else would hurt as much.

She stared hard out of the window at the cypresses that lined the grand, sweeping driveway, trying to force away the prickle of tears. 'You won't, you mean.'

'Can't, won't. What does it matter?'

'It matters to me.'

'Fine.' His voice was expressionless. 'I won't.'

The trees wavered in her vision as she lost the battle. Two weeks ago she would have blinked the tears back, pretended they weren't there, but now she made no effort to hide them. What was the point when she'd already given her own feelings away?

'I'm not your mother,' she said, though why she was arguing with him she didn't know. Was she hoping to change his mind? 'I'm not an alcoholic battling addiction. I'm just a woman who wants someone to care about her. You do understand that, don't you?'

'Of course I understand that.' Anger threaded

through his voice. 'But this isn't about my mother. This isn't about the past. It's about the choice I made for the future years ago and I'm not about to change it.'

The tears ran down her cheek, but she made no attempt to brush them away. She wanted to ask him whether he would change it for their baby's sake, except they'd already had that discussion, and besides she couldn't—wouldn't—use their child that way.

So all she said was, 'Not even for me?'

There was a heavy silence and then footsteps came from behind her. Dante's hands were suddenly on her shoulders, turning her round to face him, his expression tightening as he saw the tears running down her face.

'Stella,' he demanded roughly, something that looked like pain in the depths of his eyes. 'Why does this matter to you so very much?'

She looked up at him, lifting her chin, because even now, even here, she couldn't resist the challenge. 'Why do you think? Because you matter, Dante. You matter to me.'

His expression tightened, his fingers digging into her shoulders almost painfully. 'I told you not to care, kitten. Remember? I *told* you not to.'

She swallowed, her throat aching, everything aching. 'Too late.'

Dante could hear his own heartbeat loud and heavy in his ears, and something was cracking right down the middle of his chest, breaking him in two.

Who knew a woman's tears had the power to do that? His mother had been able to turn hers off and on, depending on what she wanted to get him to do. But there was nothing feigned about Stella's. They rolled slowly down her cheeks, one after the other, pain glowing in her silver-blue eyes.

Silly, *silly* kitten. She cared about him. *Dio,* why on earth would she go and do that? After the warning he'd given her back in Rome? After he'd dismissed all that caring nonsense and showed her that their physical connection could bridge any gap?

It was her own fault, of course. Not his. He'd been very clear about his feelings on the subject. He wasn't going to care about anyone or anything, not again, and he'd told her he wouldn't. She'd known that from the beginning.

So why the sight of her tears and the anguish in her gaze made him feel as if she really had taken that letter opener and plunged it into the centre of his chest, he had no idea.

He tried to dismiss the pain, but it wouldn't go away, and that made him angry. Made him want to crush her to him, cover her lovely, vulnerable mouth with his, make her forget her ridiculous decision to care about him, to give her pleasure instead.

But almost as soon as the impulse occurred to him and he began to pull her close her hands came up and she pushed them hard against his chest, holding herself away.

'No, Dante,' she said, hoarse and shaken. 'Not this time.'

Tension coiled in him, the sharp, restless need to do something—anything—to stop her from saying the words he so desperately did not want to hear. To take away her pain. 'You said you'd never turn me away.' His own voice sounded as rough as hers. 'That you'd never refuse me.'

'I know.' Bright determination glowed in her eyes despite the tracks of her tears. 'But that was before I knew I was in love with you, Dante Cardinali.'

Love. That damn word again. The word he'd tried to strip down over the years so that it had lost all meaning, become nothing. But he hadn't been successful, had he? Because of course it meant something.

Guilt. Pain.

'I don't want you to be in love with me,' he said viciously. 'I didn't ask for it.'

'I didn't ask for it either.' Her chin lifted higher, a challenge. 'And quite frankly the last thing in the world I want is to be in love with a man who doesn't give a damn. And yet here we are.'

His jaw was tight, his whole body stiff with tension. She was so warm against him, and so soft. All it would take would be the right touch, a kiss, and she'd melt the way she always did. He knew how to do it. He knew how to make her forget.

'So?' He slid his hands down over the delicious curve of her bottom, fitting her more closely against his hardening groin. 'It doesn't change anything.' And it wouldn't. Because he wouldn't let it.

'Dante, no.' Stella pushed harder against his chest,

her palms little points of heat on him. 'You don't understand. It changes *everything*.'

A growl escaped him. He didn't want to let her go. He wanted to keep holding her, because he had the awful suspicion that if he let her go he'd never get to hold her again. 'Why?'

Colour had risen in her cheeks, flushing her pale skin a delicate rose. She was so beautiful and yet the pain in her eyes hurt him in ways he didn't understand. 'Let me go.'

'You're going to leave, aren't you?' He couldn't stop himself from asking stupid questions, when what he should have been doing was crushing her mouth under his. 'As soon as I let you go, you're going to walk away.'

She looked vulnerable and yet there was something strong in her too, a determination he'd seen the night she'd tried to take his life. Only this time it wasn't the brittle strength of a woman forcing herself to do something she knew was wrong, it was the enduring strength of a woman knowing she would do the right thing, no matter the cost to herself. No matter her own pain.

'All I wanted was for someone to put their arms around me.' Her voice was very soft, the edges of it frayed and ragged like torn silk. 'To hold me and tell me that I was loved. But no one ever did.' Her gaze remained steady on his, a terrible knowledge glowing there. 'And Dante, if I marry you, no one ever will.'

Such simple words to have such power. It felt as

if she'd plunged not just a knife into his heart but a sword sharp enough to cut through stone.

But she was right. If he married her, if he tied her to him, she would never have that. Because he could never give it to her.

Would *never give it to her*.

No. He wouldn't. And it was a choice. He understood that much.

He'd had a choice back when he'd been a teenager and his mother had told him to go, to leave her alone. And he had. Because he'd been done with her and her constant refusal of everything he tried to do for her. Done with trying to love a woman who'd only dragged him with her because she hadn't wanted to be alone.

Who had never wanted *him*.

Because, if she had, she would have tried, wouldn't she? She would have made some kind of effort to be the kind of mother he'd needed, surely?

Ah, but that was useless to think about. Those questions had no answers and he'd never get them, because she was dead, denying him to the last.

If you hadn't walked away, things might have been different.

And that was the hell of it, wasn't it? Because he *had* walked away. And he would never know if he could have changed things if he'd stayed.

He'd never know if he could have saved her.

Guilt twisted in his heart, but he shoved it away, buried it deep.

This wasn't the same situation and Stella wasn't a

fragile, bitter addict, but the choice he had to make was still the same. And he knew he would make the same decision, because he knew exactly how this little story played out.

He would give her everything she wanted, everything that was in his power to give, except that one little piece of himself. And it wouldn't be enough for her. And eventually that would turn to bitterness and anger. It would turn to pain. It would destroy what relationship they did have, and it wouldn't only involve him and her, it would involve their child as well.

The anger inside him, the fire that never went out, flared hot and bitter.

Yes, this was her fault. She was ruining what they had with her constant need for more. And she was ruining it for their child too.

That's right. Blame her for your own cowardice. Remind you of anyone?

Dante ignored the snide voice in his head. Instead he opened his arms, letting her go and stepping back, the warmth of her body lingering against him in a way that nearly broke him.

'There,' he said, his tone acid. 'If you want to go, go. I won't stop you.'

She looked so small standing there by herself, the silky dress she wore his favourite colour, a pale, silvery blue the exact same shade as her eyes. 'So that's really the way it's going to end?' she asked quietly. 'You walking away again?'

'Does it look like I'm walking away?' His voice echoed with a bitterness and he couldn't hide it. 'No, darling, you're the one who doesn't want what I have to give.'

Her mouth trembled. 'I do want it. I just want *all* of it. I want to be loved, Dante. I want to be loved by you.'

It felt as if she'd swung that sword again, cutting through his chest, through sinew and bone, right into his heart.

'Why?' He ignored the pain, reaching for his anger instead. 'Why can't you be happy with what we have now? I'll give you everything you want. Every damn thing, Stella.'

'I know you will,' she said sadly. 'And maybe that would have been enough for me a week or so ago. But it's not enough for me now.'

'Why not?' He'd taken a step towards her before he realised what he was doing, his hands in fists at his sides. 'Why can't that be enough?'

She was framed by the window, the green of the view behind her, and there was something about it that made her seem very isolated and alone, yet at the same time it highlighted her quiet strength.

He didn't understand how she could ever have thought herself weak.

'Because I'm not the same person I was a week ago. You changed me, Dante. You made me want more. You made me think I deserve more. And I… don't want to live the rest of my life simply being content with whatever you choose to give me.' Her shoulders straightened, her jaw firmed. 'I need to be loved. I *need* it. And I don't want to have to earn it or be forever trying to change your mind to get it. I did that with my father and I don't want to do it again.'

Of course she had. And the fact that he understood her made everything worse somehow.

He felt as though he was trying to hold onto something precious that was slipping through his fingers and it took every atom of will he possessed not to go to her and take her in his arms again, to physically hold onto her so she didn't disappear. 'You'll have the baby,' he forced out through gritted teeth. 'You don't need love from me.'

But she only shook her head slowly. 'No, I won't put that on our baby. It's not fair.' Another tear rolled down her cheek. 'I'm sorry, Dante. I can't do this. I can't spend my life waiting for love from another man who'll never give it to me. I don't want that for our child either.'

Everything was slipping out of his grasp and he had no idea how to get it back. Because to get it back would mean admitting that he cared, and he didn't. He just damn well didn't.

He couldn't afford to.

He had nothing more of his heart left to give anyway.

Not even for your son or daughter?

But anger raged inside him like a bonfire, scorching everything in sight, and he didn't want to think about his child right now. What he wanted was to tell her all this was her fault, that she was the one ruining everything, that he expected better from her than ultimatums.

But he locked the furious words safely away. Smothered the bonfire with indifference. Deprived it of oxygen by slamming the door on every single feeling he had.

And it was easy. Easier than he'd expected.

'Fine.' He tried to sound lazy and casual, the way he always did. 'It's up to you, of course. But this is turning out to be more trouble than it's worth, so you'll forgive me if perhaps we put this marriage situation on hold for the time being.'

Pain flashed across her face; she knew what that tone of his meant as much as he did. And it hurt him. It flayed him alive.

But he ignored that too. Because did she seriously expect him to cave in to her demands simply because she loved him? Ridiculous.

'I understand.' Her voice was level and yet he could hear the hurt laced through it like a crack in a perfect windowpane. 'And the baby?'

'I'll buy this *palazzo*.' He gestured at the empty room, taking care not to look too closely at it as he took a hammer to the fantasies he'd been constructing about it in his head. 'You can live here until the child is born. Then we'll have to work out some other arrangements.'

Her mouth trembled as if her strength was coming to an end. 'I thought you wanted two parents for our child, Dante. I thought you wanted to live with us.'

'So did I.' He held her gaze, let her see the utter indifference in his. Because she was right about one thing: his child was better off without him. 'Seems I was mistaken.'

Sadness filled her eyes. 'So that's your response? You're going to walk away from us? Oh, Dante…'

The disappointment and hurt in her voice made him want to howl in agony. Instead, he gave a hollow laugh. 'What? You really thought I'd do anything different? Come now, kitten. You know what kind of man I am. As you've already pointed out, my child is going to suffer having me for a father anyway. Might as well live the part.' He forced himself to turn away, because he wasn't going to stand there looking at the pain on Stella's face a second longer. 'I'll get a car back to Milan. I think I'll stay there a couple of days, in fact. You can stay in Rome until the purchase of this house comes through.' He began to walk towards the exit, having to force himself to take every step. 'Don't worry, everything will be taken care of.'

'I *do* know what kind of man you are, Dante Cardinali,' Stella said from behind him, her voice echoing in the empty room. 'I only wish you did too.'

Pain reverberated through him, but he didn't turn. 'I'm sorry, kitten. That man doesn't exist.'

He didn't expect her to call after him as he walked through the door and, when she didn't, he tried not to tell himself he was disappointed.

CHAPTER TEN

DANTE SAT IN the rooftop garden of his newly bought penthouse in Milan, where he'd once envisaged putting a luxurious day-bed so he and Stella could spend some 'adult' time in any spare moments they might have while looking after their child.

But as he lolled on one of the white couches under the pergola, yet another glass of wine on the table at his elbow as the sun set over Milan, he decided that perhaps one wasn't enough. He'd get in two. After all, he'd need more than one for all the lovely women he'd be bringing up here, because of course he'd be bringing lots of women up here.

Since he wasn't getting married now, he wouldn't need to be faithful, which meant he could sleep around the way he always had.

It would have been a reassuring thought if it also hadn't filled him with a weary kind of distaste. Perhaps it meant he was getting old.

Or perhaps it means you only want her.

No, that would be ridiculous. Why would he? Stella was gone anyway, back to Rome and the penthouse suite they'd stayed at initially, just as he'd told her to. She was, after all, still pregnant with his child and the *palazzo* wasn't quite ready to accommodate her just yet.

Pain shifted in his chest so he lifted his wine glass and took another sip. Sometimes alcohol helped and sometimes it didn't.

Looked like it was going to be another day where it didn't.

A footstep made him look up from his contemplation of the view and he frowned as the tall figure of his brother stepped out from the living area and onto the rooftop.

'How did you get in?' Dante demanded.

'The front door was open.' Enzo casually strolled over and sat down on the chair opposite him.

'Nonsense. The front door has a keypad and a lock that automatically engages.'

'Fine. I had someone dismantle the lock.' There was not one ounce of shame in Enzo's expression. 'You weren't answering the door.'

Dante took a sip of his wine and scowled. 'Seems like overkill.'

'It's been five days, Dante. I was worried.'

'Why? I'm fine.' He gestured with his glass at the rooftop around them. 'As you can see.'

Enzo's golden eyes narrowed. 'You are not fine. You look like you haven't slept in days.'

'I haven't.' Dante shrugged. 'A small bout of insomnia. It's nothing.'

But his brother's gaze was sharp and Dante had the

uncomfortable sensation that Enzo could read every thought in his head.

'I had a call,' Enzo said after a moment. 'From a woman.'

Dante went very still, something clutching tightly in his chest. 'What woman?'

'I think you know which woman I mean.' His brother looked steadily at him. 'The woman expecting your child. Who's been very worried about you, regardless of the way you walked out on her.'

A spike of pain welled up inside him, leaking through the cracks in the denial he'd laid over the top of it. A denial that had been working very well the whole of the past week until now.

Probably meant he needed to drink some more.

'I don't know what woman you're talking about,' he said flatly, taking another sip.

Enzo's expression darkened. 'I thought you were a man, Dante. Not a coward.'

The denial cracked a little more and this time it was anger leaking out, a hot wave of it. And suddenly Dante lifted his glass and threw it hard against the stone wall of the parapet that bounded the garden.

It shattered, wine dripping onto the stone floor.

There was a silence, broken only by the sound of his breathing, fast and hard, as though he'd been running for days. Which he had been.

Running from the sound of Stella's voice telling him she knew what kind of man he was.

Running from the sound of his own cowardice as he'd told her that man didn't exist.

'Feel better?' Enzo asked mildly.

'No,' Dante said.

'Well.' His brother leaned back in his chair and eyed him. 'This is familiar.'

Oh, yes, he supposed it was. He remembered having a talk with Enzo just like this one when his brother had nearly lost the woman he loved. How ironic that it should be Enzo coming to talk to him now.

'Best to go away, brother mine,' Dante growled. 'I'm not in the mood.'

'Don't be ridiculous,' Enzo said, ignoring him. 'Stella is going to have your child and you're here sulking like Simon does when he's having one of his tantrums. I thought you'd at least behave better than my five-year-old.'

The sound of her name reverberated through him, striking sparks of pain through his entire body. 'Don't,' he said dangerously. 'Don't you dare say her name.'

'Why? Because it hurts you?' Enzo ignored the warning. 'You're a fool, little brother. She told me what went on—and don't worry, she only told me after I demanded she tell me everything. And I can read between the lines. You fell in love with her, and you didn't know how to deal with it, so you pushed her away.'

You fell in love with her...

The words dropped into a quiet space in Dante's head, echoing.

'You're wrong,' he forced out. 'I'm not in love with her. I'm indifferent to her.'

'Is that right? So why did you walk away? Why are you sitting here in an apparently unfurnished apartment, drinking by yourself and refusing to answer the door?' Enzo shook his head. 'You told me once that Mama had her own issues. And I can guess what they might be.' Something in his face flickered. 'I will never forgive myself for the fact that you had to deal with them alone, that I didn't come after you when Mama dragged you away.'

Another crack ran through Dante's denial, jagged and raw. 'You were young. And I coped. I was fine—'

'No,' Enzo said forcefully. 'You didn't cope. And you're not fine. If you were fine, you would be with the woman you loved and readying yourself for the birth of your first child. Instead, you're sitting here drinking, pretending you don't care when any fool can see that you care so deeply you can't deal with it.'

Dante didn't know what to say. He sat there staring at his brother, feeling the denial start to break apart inside him, and he could do nothing at all to stop it.

'She died, Enzo,' he heard himself say. 'And I couldn't save her. I walked away and let her die.'

Enzo didn't ask who he was talking about. 'Mama chose her own path and you know it. So don't let her choices dictate yours.' He paused, his golden gaze steady and sure. 'You're doing exactly what she used to do, you know that, don't you? Drowning your own pain with alcohol and pushing away the people who love you.'

Dante stared at his brother, conscious of a trickle of ice water dripping down his back. A trickle that became a flood as understanding broke over him.

Because of course Enzo was right. He *was* doing exactly what his mother had done. Drinking away the pain, refusing help. Denying the people who loved him. Hurting them, blaming them…

The way he'd hurt and blamed Stella for the simple crime of loving him and wanting to be loved in return. *Dio*, would he do the same thing to his child too?

Shame swept over him.

'I hurt her,' he said, hoarse and a bit desperate. 'I told her not to care about me and then I…blamed her for wanting more. I blamed her for ruining what we had.' He took a breath. 'It's not her fault. It's mine.'

His brother's gaze softened. 'That's a start. So what are you going to do about it?'

Dante's whole body felt tight. All he could see was the pain in Stella's lovely blue eyes and the tears on her cheeks. Tears *he'd* put there. 'What *can* I do? I walked away from her. I pretended I didn't care and then just left.'

'There's one thing you can do,' Enzo said. 'Accept that you do care and then spend every second of your life showing her exactly how much.'

Dante stared at his brother, into the face of the only other person in his life he'd ever cared about. 'How did you do it with Matilda?' he asked. 'How did you just…put everything aside and make that decision?'

Enzo lifted a shoulder. 'It was easy. I finally understood that I loved her. That her pain was more important than my own.'

'Easy.' Dante echoed mirthlessly.

But Enzo only shook his head. 'It's about acceptance, brother. Not that river in Egypt.'

It was a lame joke, but then his brother had never been very good at humour.

Just as Dante had never been very good at acceptance.

'All I ever wanted was for someone to put their arms around me and tell me I was loved...'

She'd told him that and it was such a simple thing to give her. Only his heart. And what did his heart matter anyway? Who was he holding onto it for? There was no one else he wanted to give it to but her and, if she took it and ripped it into shreds, what of it? There would be pain and he'd had pain before.

Besides, he owed it to her for the way he'd walked out. He owed her an apology. And if she threw it back in his face it wouldn't be anything he didn't deserve.

And, apart from anything else, he wanted to see her shattered sky eyes just once more.

'I think,' he said. 'That I suddenly need to be in Rome. Urgently.'

Enzo eyed him. 'It's nearly midnight.'

Dante surged up out of his chair. The denial had cracked apart and melted away as if it had never been, leaving nothing but an intense, aching hunger he knew was never going to go away. 'I don't care. I have to go now.'

Enzo snorted. 'Good thing I got the helicopter ready to go, then, isn't it?'

Stella was asleep and dreaming. It was one of the lovely and yet terribly painful dreams that had been plaguing her for the past week, where she would feel strong arms around her and a muscular, power-ful body at her back keeping her warm. And a rich, dark voice would whisper in her ear, except she could never hear the words. There were too indistinct.

The dream hurt and always ended the same way, with her waking up alone, a deep, intense yearn-ing in her heart for something she was never going to have.

She hated those dreams.

In fact, as she lay curled up in the bed she'd once shared with Dante, she thought she was having one now, because warm arms slid around her, drawing her against an achingly familiar body. Hot, muscu-lar and smelling of sandalwood, folding around her and keeping her safe.

She gave a little moan of resistance and shivered as she felt lips nuzzle her ear, her whole body falling into longing as that dark voice began to whisper the words she never seemed to hear.

Except right now, alone in her bed, she heard them.

'Stella Montefiore,' the dream said. 'I have some-thing to tell you.' Those arms tightened around her, holding her fast. 'You are wanted. You are loved. And you are loved by me.'

Stella trembled. Was she awake? Or was this still a dream? Because, if it was a dream, she didn't want to wake up.

But the voice was still speaking, that familiar voice that made her want to cry. 'I'm sorry, kitten,' Dante murmured. 'I'm so sorry for the way I left you. For all the terrible things I said to you. I've got no excuse for them other than the one you probably already know. I was afraid. I didn't want to feel anything, I didn't want to care. But I did care. I cared about you.'

She shuddered, not wanting move or speak in case the dream disappeared, a sob collecting in her throat.

'You told me you knew what kind of man I am,' he went on, 'but all I knew was that I was the man who'd walked out on his mother because she wouldn't give me even one single sign that she loved me. And then she died. And maybe if I hadn't walked out, if I hadn't wanted to be loved so badly, I might have been there to save her.'

Stella couldn't keep still any more.

She turned over, heart bursting in her chest, half-terrified of what she would see—that it wouldn't be the man she wanted, just that awful dream again, and she'd be left with nothing.

But it wasn't a dream.

Dante was lying in the bed, his eyes gleaming and black in the dim room, his expression stripped bare. He was in his usual suit trousers and shirt, yet his shirt was creased and had clearly seen better days, and his normally clean-shaven jaw was dark with stubble.

He looked tired and worn and desperate, and still the most beautiful man she'd ever seen.

'You're here,' she croaked, reaching out a shaking hand to touch his beloved face. 'How did you get here?'

Dante didn't smile, only looked into her eyes. 'I had a visit from my brother. He told me that you'd called him because you were worried about me.'

She was still shaking and she couldn't stop. Couldn't stop from running her fingers along his cheekbone either, his skin warm and real beneath her fingertips. 'I did and I was. And I'm not sorry I called him.'

'I'm not sorry either.' Dante's gaze was dark, fathomless. 'Enzo told me I was doing exactly what my mother had done, sitting there blaming everyone else for my pain and pushing away the people I loved. Hurting them…' He stopped. 'You wanted more from me and I hurt you. I was selfish and I blamed you.'

'Dante—'

'No, you were right to want more, Stella. Do you understand? You were right.' He lifted his hand and caught hers where it was pressed to his cheek and held it there. 'I needed to stop pretending I didn't care. To accept that I did. I needed to stop thinking only of myself, stop turning into my own damn mother.' Gently he lowered her hand and kissed the tips of her fingers. 'And, most important of all, I needed to realise that I was in love with you. Because I am, Stella Montefiore. I think I've been in love with you since the moment I woke up to find you pointing a gun at my head.'

Her chest went tight, her heart so full it felt as though it was pressing on the sides of her ribs. 'Is that why you're here?'

'Yes. I wanted to apologise.' The ghost of his charming smile turned his mouth, but there was something desperate in his dark eyes. 'And to tell you that I will love our child too, with the same desperation with which I love you. And also that my heart is yours, if you want it. But, if you don't, I'll leave you in peace. I won't ever bother you with it again.'

A tear leaked out despite her best intentions and, because her voice didn't work, she leaned forward and gave him her answer by brushing her mouth over his instead.

And instantly he moved, his arms going around her, holding her hard against him and then rolling her beneath him.

'You know that's it, don't you?' he growled, intense gold flames burning in the depths of his eyes. 'That means I'm never letting you go.'

Stella got her arms free then raised them and wound them around his neck, holding onto him as tightly as he was holding on to her. 'I don't want you to let me go. I want you to hold me for ever, Dante Cardinali.'

'And if I don't?'

Stella thought about it. 'Then I might be forced to kill you.'

Dante gave her a sudden fierce, brilliant smile. 'Don't kill me, kitten. Love me instead.'

So that was what she did.

EPILOGUE

'WHERE IS MY COUSIN?' Simon Cardinali demanded, fixing his uncle with a fierce stare.

Enzo, who was standing outside Stella's hospital door and holding Simon's hand, frowned. 'Simon, where are your manners? You know better than that.'

The little boy pulled a face. 'Sorry, Papa,' he muttered. 'But…where is my cousin, *please*?'

Dante gazed down at his small nephew and grinned. 'She's asleep.'

'But I've got a present,' Simon complained.

'She's still a baby,' Dante explained reasonably. 'And she needs her sleep. She can see your present tomorrow.'

'Tomorrow?' Simon looked aghast. 'But that's *for ever*!'

An exasperated expression crossed Enzo's face. 'I'm going to take you back to your mother.' He gave Dante a glance—he'd already congratulated his brother on the new addition to the Cardinali family. 'How is Stella?'

'She's doing well,' Dante said, and she was. The

birth had been tough going, but his kitten had been strong. Stronger than he'd been, at any rate.

'And Sofia?'

Dante thought about his daughter and grinned like a lunatic. 'She's perfect.'

Enzo gave a brisk nod. 'Well, you get some rest too. You look like hell.'

Dante didn't feel like hell. He felt incredible. As if he could do anything.

After his brother and nephew had gone, he went silently back into the private hospital room where Stella and their new daughter were sleeping.

Sofia was awake in her crib, her dark eyes—that he knew would end up being silver-blue, just like her mother's—staring up into his. And he found he could only look at her for a couple of moments at a time because it was either that or his heart would burst out of sheer joy.

He was going to have to learn how to deal with that.

Dante made sure the soft blanket was pulled snugly around his daughter and that she was quiet before moving over to the bed where his wife lay.

Stella blinked sleepily as he sat down beside her and smiled, her hand reaching for his.

He took it, the joy inside him becoming complete.

'You were amazing, my kitten,' he said quietly. 'I never knew how much strength it took to bring a new life into the world.'

Stella's smile deepened. 'You were pretty amazing yourself.'

Dante gave a rueful laugh. 'I did not handle it well.'

'You only swore and shouted twice. And you didn't threaten anyone with death, not once.'

Stella was being kind. Being with his wife while she'd been in pain and he'd been unable to help her had been one of the most difficult things he'd ever had to do.

'You set me a great example,' he said. 'I got my strength from you.'

'Because you were with me.' Her fingers tightened around his. 'We got our strength from each other.'

And she was right, they had. Because they loved each other.

Dante lifted his wife's hand to his mouth and kissed it. 'I love you, Stella Cardinali.'

Her smile was the one she kept for him and him alone. 'I will never get tired of hearing you say that.'

He turned her hand over and kissed her palm, staring into her shattered sky eyes. 'That's good, because I plan to keep saying it every day for the rest of our lives.'

And he did.

Because, as dedicated as he'd once been to being a reckless playboy who didn't feel a thing, he was even more dedicated to being a loving husband and father.

And, as it turned out, he was very good at that.

He was very good indeed.

* * * * *

If you enjoyed
Claiming His One-Night Child
by Jackie Ashenden,
why not look out for the first instalment in her
Shocking Italian Heirs duet?
Demanding His Hidden Heir
Available now!

And why not explore
these other Jackie Ashenden stories,
from our fantastic DARE series?

Ruined
Destroyed
King's Price
King's Rule
King's Ransom
Available now!

#3745 HIS CINDERELLA'S ONE-NIGHT HEIR
One Night With Consequences
by Lynne Graham

Billionaire Dante's fake relationship with Belle was supposed
to last only two weeks. But one night of seduction in Paris will
change the course of their convenient arrangement forever, with
the news that Belle is carrying his baby!

#3746 HIS FORBIDDEN PREGNANT PRINCESS
by Maisey Yates

King Luca's plan to handpick a husband for his innocent stepsister,
Sophia, backfires wildly when the forbidden desire simmering
between them explodes into life! It must never happen again.
Until Luca discovers Sophia is pregnant with his heir...

#3747 SHEIKH'S ROYAL BABY REVELATION
Secret Heirs of Billionaires
by Annie West

When Sheikh Ashraf was kidnapped alongside Tori, their
desperation to escape led to passionate oblivion. Rescued the
next day, Ash was never able to discover Tori's fate. Now he's
finally found her. But—startlingly—she's had his son!

#3748 CONSEQUENCES OF A HOT HAVANA NIGHT
Passion in Paradise
by Louise Fuller

Rum distiller Kitty is shocked to that learn that César, the elusive
stranger she shared one explosive night with, is actually her boss.
But that's nothing compared to Kitty's latest realisation... She's
pregnant!

HPCNM0819RA

#3749 THE GREEK'S VIRGIN TEMPTATION
by Susan Stephens

Jilted bride Kimmie is adamant that her honeymoon party will still go ahead. Her celebration leads her to billionaire Kristof...who tempts Kimmie to share her unspent wedding night with him!

#3750 SHOCK MARRIAGE FOR THE POWERFUL SPANIARD
Conveniently Wed!
by Cathy Williams

Rafael has one aim: to find Sofia—the woman due to inherit the company he's poised to take over—and propose a mutually beneficial marriage! But this Spaniard's potent need for Sofia is unexpected—and changes everything...

#3751 IRRESISTIBLE BARGAIN WITH THE GREEK
by Julia James

Heiress Talia is stunned when Luke, the stranger she spent one earth-shattering night with, returns! He offers Talia a job to save her family home... She can't turn down the arrangement—or deny their still-powerful chemistry!

#3752 REDEEMED BY HER INNOCENCE
by Bella Frances

Ruthless Nikos won't risk his company to save Jacquelyn's struggling bridal boutique. But he will give her the best night of her life! Could untouched Jacquelyn's sensual surrender be this dark-hearted Greek's redemption?

Get 4 FREE REWARDS!

We'll send you 2 FREE Books
<u>plus</u> 2 FREE Mystery Gifts.

Harlequin Presents® books feature a sensational and sophisticated world of international romance where sinfully tempting heroes ignite passion.

FREE Value Over $20

YES! Please send me 2 FREE Harlequin Presents® novels and my 2 FREE gifts (gifts are worth about $10 retail). After receiving them, if I don't wish to receive any more books, I can return the shipping statement marked "cancel." If I don't cancel, I will receive 6 brand-new novels every month and be billed just $4.55 each for the regular-print edition or $5.80 each for the larger-print edition in the U.S., or $5.49 each for the regular-print edition or $5.99 each for the larger-print edition in Canada. That's a savings of at least 11% off the cover price! It's quite a bargain! Shipping and handling is just 50¢ per book in the U.S. and $1.25 per book in Canada.* I understand that accepting the 2 free books and gifts places me under no obligation to buy anything. I can always return a shipment and cancel at any time. The free books and gifts are mine to keep no matter what I decide.

Choose one: ☐ **Harlequin Presents®**
Regular-Print
(106/306 HDN GNWY)

☐ **Harlequin Presents®**
Larger-Print
(176/376 HDN GNWY)

Name (please print)

Address   Apt. #

City   State/Province   Zip/Postal Code

Mail to the **Reader Service:**
IN U.S.A.: P.O. Box 1341, Buffalo, NY 14240-8531
IN CANADA: P.O. Box 603, Fort Erie, Ontario L2A 5X3

Want to try 2 free books from another series? Call 1-800-873-8635 or visit www.ReaderService.com.

---

*Terms and prices subject to change without notice. Prices do not include sales taxes, which will be charged (if applicable) based on your state or country of residence. Canadian residents will be charged applicable taxes. Offer not valid in Quebec. This offer is limited to one order per household. Books received may not be as shown. Not valid for current subscribers to Harlequin Presents books. All orders subject to approval. Credit or debit balances in a customer's account(s) may be offset by any other outstanding balance owed by or to the customer. Please allow 4 to 6 weeks for delivery. Offer available while quantities last.

Your Privacy—The Reader Service is committed to protecting your privacy. Our Privacy Policy is available online at www.ReaderService.com or upon request from the Reader Service. We make a portion of our mailing list available to reputable third parties that offer products we believe may interest you. If you prefer that we not exchange your name with third parties, or if you wish to clarify or modify your communication preferences, please visit us at www.ReaderService.com/consumerchoice or write to us at Reader Service Preference Service, P.O. Box 9062, Buffalo, NY 14240-9062. Include your complete name and address.

HP19R3

She looked up at César. "It's positive."

His expression didn't change by so much as a tremor.

"I'm pregnant."

She knew that these tests were 99 percent accurate, but somehow saying the words out loud made it feel more real. It was there—in her hand. She was going to have a baby.

Only, the person who was supposed to be the father, supposed to be there with her, was no longer around.

Her heartbeat had slowed; she felt as if she was in a dream. "I'm pregnant," she said again.

César's grip tightened around her hand, and as she met his gaze she felt her legs wilt. His eyes were so very green, and for a moment all she could think was that they should be brown.

Her head was swimming. It had taken five years, but most days she was content with her life. She still regretted Jimmy's death, but the acute pain, that hollowed-out ache of despair, had faded a few years ago. Only now this news had reawakened old emotions.

He caught her arm. "You need to sit down."

Still holding her hand, he led her into the living room. She sat down on the sofa. The first shock was starting to wear off and panic was starting to ripple over her skin.

"I don't understand how this could happen."

When she and Jimmy had started trying for a baby, he had been so keen he'd taken a fertility test and everything had been normal. She'd been about to get herself checked out when he fell ill, and then there had been too much going on, other more urgent tests to take, and so each time she wasn't pregnant she had blamed herself—her periods had always been irregular. Only now it seemed as though it hadn't been her.

César sat down beside her. "I'm pretty sure it happened the usual way."

She stared at him dazedly. Her head was a muddle of emotions, but he was so calm. So reasonable.

"You haven't asked me," she said slowly, "if the baby could be someone else's."

In a way, that was more of a shock than her pregnancy. With hindsight, her late period, her sudden craving for fruit juice and her heightened relentless fatigue all pointed to one obvious explanation, but she knew it was a question most men in his situation would have asked.

He leaned back a little, studying her face. There was an expression in his eyes that she couldn't fathom.

For a moment he didn't reply, and then he shrugged. "What happened between us isn't something I've found easy to forget. I'd like to believe that you feel the same way. But if you think there's any question over my paternity, now would be a good time to say so."

She shook her head. "There hasn't been anyone but you." Her eyes flicked to his face. "And, yes, I feel the same way."

As she spoke, some of the tension in her shoulders lifted. They hadn't planned for this to happen, to bring new life into the world, and they might not love one another, but those few heated moments had been fierce and important for both of them, and she was glad that this child had been conceived out of such extraordinary mutual passion.

"I don't regret it," she said abruptly. "What we did or what's happened."

Her heart swelled. She had wanted and waited for this baby for so long, and suddenly all those other tests, with their accusatory ghostly white rectangles, seemed to grow vague and unsubstantial.

"Well, it's a little late for regrets." He paused. "This baby isn't going anywhere. What matters now is what happens next."

Don't miss
Consequences of a Hot Havana Night
available September 2019 wherever
Harlequin® Presents books and ebooks are sold.

www.Harlequin.com